COUNTERFEIT

Also by Guillermo Valcárcel

Shadows Across America

COUNTERFEIT

GUILLERMO VALCÁRCEL

Translated by Kit Maude

amazon crossing

This is a work of fiction. Names, characters, organizations, places, events, and incidents are either products of the author's imagination or are used fictitiously. Any resemblance to actual persons, living or dead, or actual events is purely coincidental.

Previously published as *El conseguidor* by SUMA, an imprint of Penguin Random House Grupo Editorial, in Latin America in 2015. Translated from Spanish by Kit Maude. First published in English by AmazonCrossing in 2019.

Published by AmazonCrossing, Seattle
www.apub.com

ISBN-13: 9781542042215
ISBN-10: 1542042216

Cover design by Philip Pascuzzo

Printed in the United States of America

COUNTERFEIT

Prologue

There comes a moment at the end of the night, when the sun is just about to peek over the horizon, that two cities come face to face: the daytime one, with its routines that lend a sense of security to the lives of the majority, and the nocturnal underworld, where lost children lurk, shady business is done, and the darkest desires can be satisfied, so long as you have the money to pay.

The man in the boots passed through the curtain that shielded the club from the sunlight outside without taking off his coat or sunglasses. Inside, several hazy groups were still on the dance floor, being watched attentively by figures sitting on sofas. The bartender gave a smile of recognition at the man in the boots and poured a whiskey without saying a word. The man's expression relaxed, and he sat for a moment on a stool, leaning on the practically deserted bar. He downed his drink, still holding his bag. It was just a crummy shopping bag, but he gripped it tight like his life depended on it. The warmth of the alcohol running down his throat gave him enough energy to move on to the bathroom. He left a ten-euro note on the table without looking up, got down from his stool, stumbled, and felt a warm stream of blood run down his leg into his boot, where it puddled around his foot. He was glad to be wearing the boots; they hid the blood from his wound. He checked his pants, afraid that it might show, but in the darkness it couldn't be seen through the thick fabric.

He had to get back out into the sunlight, find a car, and get away as fast as he could, before they could track him down. He needed to disappear and, once he was safe, get in touch with his partner, find Xavi, and get a name. Then he'd try to bargain for his life. At first, he'd considered fighting back, but it was useless. These people seemed to have unlimited resources. If he wanted to save himself, he'd have to give them something. His partner, maybe, that blubbering coward. If they'd asked him, he'd have happily turned the guy in. Yeah, if push came to shove, he'd give them his partner and Xavi. Where the hell had the other guy come from? He didn't know, but he'd be willing to track him down. He'd have no trouble doing it. Yes, he said again to calm himself down, he'd find whatever it was they wanted. He'd work for them, and if they asked, he'd give up all three of them: his partner, Xavi, and that guy with them. What was his name? He'd serve them up on a silver platter. But first he needed to disappear. If they found him now, after last night, there'd be no escape. He was in no position to make a deal. Yes, he needed to disappear; then he'd make contact with them and arrange to save himself. And with the vague idea that he still had a chance, already making half-baked plans to negotiate with the people who had tried to kill him, he went into the men's room.

Covered in filthy dark stains, the bathroom stank. The floor was sopping wet after the long night. In the glow from the only working light, a couple of men were making some kind of exchange, but they moved on when they saw him. One of them recognized him and mumbled something, but the man in the boots, preoccupied with his forthcoming journey, barely noticed. He went into the first stall. The toilet bowl was clogged with paper and piss, its malodourous contents close to overflowing from the bowl. He lowered the lid and emptied out the contents of the bag: a new white shirt still in its packaging, a tube of superglue, white packing tape, medicinal alcohol, a roll of cling film, and a pair of cheap sunglasses.

Only then did he dare to take off his coat and check his shirt—fuck, this was his favorite shirt. It was torn on one side and soaked in blood. Underneath was a clean wound running right through him. He hunched over in pain. He wouldn't be so lucky next time. Right now what he needed more than anything was something for the pain.

He took a deep breath, used his torn shirt to wipe away the blood as best he could, opened the bottle of alcohol, and emptied it into the wound, stifling a scream. While his skin bubbled bright red under a flow that hadn't yet been staunched, he opened the wound with one hand and bit the top off the tube of glue. He ran the nozzle around the edge of the wound, trying to keep the glue from getting inside. The blood surged over it. Then he peeled cling film from the roll and wrapped it around his skin, making sure that it stuck to the glue firmly enough to hold, before doing several more passes to make a strange kind of corset. The bleeding seemed to have stopped, and he felt a little more stable, although he couldn't breathe comfortably. He reinforced the bandage with the packing tape until it felt rigid, and he grimaced as he thought, *This is going to be hell to take off.*

He painfully pulled on the new shirt; changed his sunglasses; put the stained clothes, coat, and packaging in the bag; and hid it all behind the toilet. Then he headed back outside.

The glare from the sun caught him off guard. Trying to act naturally, he mingled with the morning shoppers, hoping his strained looks and ashen skin weren't too obvious. He lurched to the entrance of an abandoned-looking building and went in carefully. The darkness swallowed him as he slipped under the stairs and took off his glasses. After waiting until his eyes had grown accustomed to the dark, he went into an office. Inside, there was only a faint trace of blood on the wall and a loose cable. He swore quietly and felt behind the furniture without finding anything. When he looked at his hand, he saw that it wasn't covered in dust. The place had been searched very recently. They might still be there. He stopped; coming back had been a dangerous move. He went back out into the hallway. He decided against the way he'd come in and instead climbed through a window onto an interior patio—several bedsheets were hanging above him, evidence that a few people still lived here—and then forced open a wooden shutter on the other side. He headed to the door of the neighboring building and managed to get out into the street opposite, thinking that would be enough to throw off anyone who was following him. But if anyone was, he reasoned, they'd have attacked him at the door.

On a quiet street, he thanked his lucky stars at finding a parked Opel Kadett, a model rarely seen these days. It was one of his favorites: easy to steal. He opened the door without much difficulty, and soon enough he'd hot-wired it. Sitting back up, he heard an approaching motorcycle. Why hadn't he heard it earlier? The driver parked next to him, and the passenger got off and opened the car door.

"Get out."

Aware of how weak he was, the man tried to kick his assailant away as he made for the other door. He reached out for the door and managed to get it open, but the kid was already on top of him. The attacker pinned him down and tried to shove a knife into his side but was surprised to find it slip off the tape. The man in the boots took advantage of the second this gave him to slip away and got most of his body outside. The boy tried to grab his legs but took a kick to the chin that left him momentarily stunned. The man fell onto the asphalt and tried to spin around to get up. Now he needed to keep running. He sensed the presence of the other rider before he saw him. The second man had ditched the motorcycle and leaped over the hood of the car to clean up his partner's mess. The last thing the man in the boots heard was an iron bar cracking his skull. The blow killed him immediately. Just to make sure, the second rider hit him a few more times until the man's forehead crumpled into his left eye and a dark puddle began spreading over the concrete. The driver took a few photos with his phone, and the pair mounted the bike, worried about the scene they'd made in broad daylight.

"Fuck you, tough guy."

"Shut up, idiot. We didn't get anything out of him—we're fucked."

"They knew he wasn't going to talk. But there's another one, isn't there?"

"Yeah, let's pray he knows something."

"Did you get the photos?"

"Of course."

They sped off, leaving only silence and emptiness behind. Their place was taken by a small car coming in the other direction. When the car's driver realized that his way was blocked by the Kadett's open door, he honked his horn and eventually got out in annoyance, looking for the moron who'd left his car with the doors dangling open like a donkey's ears. *I should just have knocked the door off!* Then he discovered the body and was met with a sight he wouldn't soon be able to forget.

1

On Sunday mornings, stalls and shops along certain streets in the Old Quarter of Madrid teemed with avid antiques lovers. El Rastro, one of the largest and busiest urban markets in the world, opened up to tourists like a prostitute determined to make her fortune, all false smiles and bustling jubilation. You never knew what you might find. Early in the morning, when it was still dark out and groups of young people were coming back after a night out, some of them shrouded in a tired, deathly pallor, connoisseurs could still come across good finds and genuine bargains. As was true of almost everything in life, you just had to know where and how to look.

In collectors' circles, there was a profession that specialized in difficult commissions, generally personal in nature, a collective that had little time for scruples or legalities. These individuals were known euphemistically as "scouts" or "salvagers." Jota knew them well. In fact, he was one of them. He spent most of his days among the dust and old objects. Now that dark, dreamlike world was disappearing, washed away by the ominous digital tidal wave sweeping across the globe. The internet's high-definition images made things look cleaner and more vibrant; everything was clearer and seemingly more substantial but less real. Globalization soon had an impact on the collectors' market, making it into one big searchable, downloadable web page. Prices went up, and rare items became a lot easier to find. Everything was connected to everything else. International supply chains fulfilled orders. Now the only barrier to entry was money. But in the art market, that was never truly a barrier at all.

There were barely any survivors from the time before the internet, people who had once had it all—or at least had felt that it was within their reach but who now lived haunted by the shadow of what might have been. Jota still had a reputation. He was still the guy you went to with impossible requests, and his scars and two hidden tattoos reminded him that things had once been different, that what he did still meant something.

The shabbier streets of the Rastro, where elderly people spread blankets across the ground and sold whatever they could find, weren't so attractive to tourists. This was Jota's world, where the vendors recognized him and always said hello, some with respect, others harboring a tinge of melancholy. He wore an old leather jacket and scruffy but comfortable clothing: a flannel shirt and jeans. He was handsome but made no effort with his appearance; gradually, he had stopped caring. He looked younger than his forty-five years, but his features were worldly—or rather world weary. Jota walked along inspecting wares without acknowledging the greetings. He was looking for something specific, acting with the confidence of someone who knew the terrain. "So this is what it's come to," he murmured in a resigned voice, sifting through junk in a large secondhand store. Eventually, he found a torso from an old doll.

Now that he'd found what he was looking for, he headed home by a street parallel to the main one leading to the famous Plaza Mayor, making his way through twisting alleys and passages full of fashionable nightclubs where tourists and young people gathered to drink. He went along under the somber gazes of centuries-old buildings with misleading facades that belied the modern apartments now sitting behind them. The fronts of these buildings were the only genuine thing about them, decorative touches to preserve the illusion of permanence. That was how his job felt these days, just like his world and the entire city: fake or sold off for a pittance. The young designers who stared at him from behind their thick glasses saw him as an example of the authenticity they were superficially attracted to. Like their decorative vinyl records, they were trying to be something they weren't, something they didn't even understand. It was all part of a game they called "vintage."

Jota let himself into a large run-down apartment in a building in the Old Quarter. It had the high ceilings, wallpaper, smoke-stained plaster moldings, doors with glass and dark wooden frames, and sinister hallways paved with geometric tiles typical of old houses, floors that concealed voices silenced long ago. The furniture was a mixture of styles and periods; it looked like an antiques warehouse, the result of years of searches and misunderstandings. He went into a room set up as a workshop, turned on a powerful table lamp, and put the doll torso in the pool of light before starting to carefully take it apart. He discarded some rotted string he found inside and replaced it with similar material extracted from a torso in much worse condition. Then he added the arms and legs he'd already prepared to make a strange-looking cadaver. He picked up a paintbrush and a magnifying glass and delicately added a pair of eyes. Puffing on a cigarette, he studied a set of doll's clothes he was aging artificially on a heater. Then he cautiously burned the hems with the butt before applying varnish to the lashless eyes. He picked up another head, broken off at the neck, and removed its eyelashes. An old doll was beginning to take shape.

When he was done, Jota headed for the store that had commissioned the Mariquita Perez doll. The antiquarian kept the window display fairly extravagant, but indoors it was so dark you could barely see. The buyer received her doll in its original box with contained excitement. After duly asking permission to take it out of its packaging, she proceeded to inspect the joints and the seams where the real hair met the head. After a long and careful examination, she declared herself satisfied and held out her hand to Jota, who had been observing the process with studied indifference. He took the hand listlessly, and the buyer then leaned over the table to examine the certificate of authenticity.

After the customer had left, he smoked a cigarette in the doorway and spoke briefly to the owner of the store. Then he went, having counted his payment a second time. He didn't seem to have any particular destination in mind, but his legs always took him to the same small, shabby antiques shop. Its entrance was half-hidden by its wares, stuffed full of objects that filtered the light into golden rays; the accumulation of clothes racks, wardrobes, iron bicycles, and old uniforms gave the shop a timeless air. In the back, in front of a closed door that led to the office, Jota found a man sitting at a cast-iron garden table, possibly made in the fifties, on which he was organizing invoices into a plastic folder.

The man, Adolfo, didn't bother to look up when Jota came in; he recognized the sound of his footsteps and allowed himself a familiar smile. Jota saw it, but neither of them said a word until Adolfo broke the silence, continuing with his accounts as he spoke.

"So you sold it?"

"Yeah, here's your share," Jota said, holding out a few notes, clearly trying to interrupt what his friend and partner was doing.

Adolfo sighed and pushed away the bills. Then he looked up. "No trouble? She just bought it?"

"Yes," Jota said, lighting a cigarette.

"She didn't want any more proof? She's not going to find an expert?"

"In the end, her brother-in-law came along. He arranged the whole deal. A cocky amateur. The woman was dazzled—she really thought it was the same doll from her childhood. She even started to notice details that weren't there. We don't even know if she ever actually had one, so there was no point trying to fool her with anything like that. She did that all on her own. I suppose that at her age one needs to believe in something."

"You know, these days you're not allowed to smoke in the workplace."

"Sure, *you're* not allowed. I'm just passing through. Anything new come up?"

"Why do you always have to be such a dick?" Adolfo said, his attention having returned to the papers on the table. "A couple of things came in. Are you really going to make me look for them now? I'm just about to close up."

"Whatever. If you don't have anything for me, I'll go do something else and leave you in peace. But don't come looking for me later."

Adolfo started to search through the pile of papers on his table. Jota took a critical look at his old friend: he was worn out, defeated by his past. Jota's spine began to itch as he reflected on their shared routine of many years. Was he just as worn out? Probably, but in a different way, not because of a failed marriage. His failures had been very different. Nonetheless, they had both been cowed by a life that had broken them just when they'd thought they were coming out on top. The difference was that Jota didn't lock himself away in a shop. He wasn't trying to hide behind piles of paperwork. He looked at his friend and felt a flurry of sincere affection for him. It was this affection that kept him coming back after all these years, taking more interest in his friend's life than was necessary, much more than Adolfo knew. Jota would never say anything about it or even ask how he was doing. They never discussed their emotions because they'd been raised in a world where boys were taught at a young age that men didn't cry. The moment the first hint of fuzz began to appear on their faces: "Remember that," his father had said between slaps. "Men don't cry."

"I have a collector looking for an iron cross from the Eastern front with a guarantee of authenticity."

"An iron cross. You can find them in any old military antiques store. Why did he come to you?"

"There are detailed instructions. The guy sounds like he knows what he's talking about; this won't be an easy job."

"It doesn't matter. There aren't any iron crosses around here anymore—only a few from the Blue Division, and they've all been identified. You won't find anything new here outside of an auction. They're not worth faking—they're too easy to verify. Nothing doing."

"What about somewhere else, in Germany maybe?"

"These days, the good stuff is in the Baltic states. Some of the pieces there have been hidden for fifty years."

"Then I'll talk to someone who specializes in imports. Rafa or Martín."

"Rafa's a thief, and Martín doesn't know shit. They'll both rob you blind, and on top of that Martín will try to screw you with a fake."

"Fuck, so you're the only one anyone can do business with. Is that it? Why don't you get back into imports?"

"I'm telling you the commission game is a bust. There's no profit to be had. What's the other one?"

Adolfo picked up a handwritten note. "I got a call from Morgades Antiques and Art, but they wanted to speak to you. I didn't know that this was your office now."

"And you're my secretary. Morgades Art? Do you know who it was?"

"Well, I imagine it was Morgades's daughter—the old man died ten years ago."

"And she wanted to speak to me?"

"She wants you to find something for her. She has a wealthy client."

"They didn't get wealthy by spreading it around."

Clara Morgades: the social climber, aging daughter of a withered alcoholic who filled her head with ambition while simultaneously leaving her out on the street. Jota remembered Morgades from long ago. He'd only met her in passing, but she had blonde, nearly platinum hair that gave her an angelic look. She'd come looking for her father in bars; she was paying his debts before she'd even left school. At the time she might have been worthy of pity, or so Jota thought. Who wasn't worthy of compassion before the world toughened them up? Morgades had left home to live with her first partner before she'd turned eighteen. He'd been thirty-six and left his wife and son for her. After that, he'd paid the old man's bills. Who could blame her? What other choice did a woman like her have? And who could blame him? She was more than beautiful—she was something else, and sweet, too, a little puppy who hid in his shadow and learned the trade while she kept his bed warm. But of course you could blame him; he knew very well what he was doing. It had taken Morgades a while to smell the coffee and ditch him, just long enough to learn everything he knew. From then on, she'd been unstoppable, but she'd never worked with Jota, who was already an institution when she was just starting out. *Best to have nothing to do with her*, he'd said to himself more than once. She was dangerous. Was she aware that her first lover went mad after she left and ended up begging in the street? Yes, of course she was; it was the price he had to pay for being with her in the first place. It was the same with the partners who followed: they always got tangled up in dodgy schemes from which she walked away scot-free and in a better position than ever. But then Morgades had disappeared many years ago; even Adolfo had never met her.

"I never had the pleasure when they lived there," Adolfo said, shaking Jota out of his rumination.

"Lucky for you."

"Does that mean that I'm not going to be a part of this deal?"

"Who says I'm going to take it?"

Adolfo smiled sardonically. Jota got up and put the cigarette out in a marble ashtray. The dealer wrinkled his nose.

"This is worth eighty euros. Are you planning on buying it?"

"Yes, I like it. Take it out of your cut for the commission. I'm going to see Richard."

"About Morgades?"

"How long has it been since we last heard from her? She's never good news, a bad omen."

"More so than you?"

"Almost as much as you."

Jota smiled ironically, but it wasn't returned. His partner no longer reacted to his jokes. He might put up with one or two, but then he'd go back to his work like a boy who'd forgotten how to play. Jota remembered when he was different. Everything had been different. He asked a final question merely to be polite.

"How are Miriam and the girls?"

"Fine, fine. Miriam's taking some vacation time to be with the girls so they won't be at home alone. We don't like them spending their days here. It's no place for them."

"Sounds good. Say hello to her from me."

"Of course. She always asks after you."

Accepting the white lie, Jota left. His old friends hid themselves away, turning their backs onto the abyss as though it weren't there at all, clinging to a fading reality in the secret hope that they'd die before it had gone entirely and they'd have to face a world they didn't understand. A faceless world that would eat up those whose new ideas had long been exhausted. He took the last cigarette from the pack, thinking about Morgades and the stains left behind as she tried to get on in life.

Richard's gym was large and modern, with deafening music in the weight room and several different classes full of sweaty people. People who'd paid for their memberships in the hope of getting the impossible: more life, health, an escape. Richard was a survivor, and this was his profession. He'd seen several different generations pass through his facilities and had grown into a neighborhood legend. He spent his life there now, more out of habit than need. When exercise became fashionable and the younger generations started to venerate their bodies, he'd paid to enlarge his space, and it appeared to have been a success. The economic crisis didn't affect everyone equally. But Richard was an old friend, a loyal one, and that was something that, as Jota well knew, couldn't be bought. He finished his cigarette before going in. The girl at reception recognized him and got up immediately.

"Good afternoon. I'll let Richard know you're here."

"Thank you."

She hurried off, and Jota looked around the place, listening to the relentless music, almost tasting the smell of liniment, peering dubiously at the energy drink dispensers. They even sold sports apparel. Richard knew every trick in the book. It may have been his greatest talent: knowing what to do with the cards he'd been dealt. He soon appeared, flanked by the girl. He was an impressive size, and his perfectly toned body, now beginning to reveal its years, lent him a surprisingly respectable air. He hugged Jota like a brother.

"Fuck me—it's about time you dropped by!"

"Yeah, well, I'm scared of you."

"Damn, what a kidder. So what have you got for me? I'd love to think you just dropped by to say hello, but I know you."

"Is this how you treat all your friends?"

"I'm right, aren't I?"

"Of course. Let's go to your lair."

Richard fussed around the office trying to tidy up a little, but Jota paid the mess no mind. The small, dark room with dirty cream walls seemed to exist simply to set off the rest of the place. Buzzing extractor fans lined the window, which looked out onto an interior courtyard. It was strange to think that Richard spent any time in this dank environment, as though he were trying to bring back the old days. Richard had built a monument to modernity, the kind that the kids who went there to train idolized and his girlfriends embodied, but he locked himself away in this dark office, hiding from his own success. Jota looked curiously out the window and started to smoke, keeping his cigarette outside. Eventually, he asked his question.

"Do you remember Morgades's daughter?"

"Is that a trick question?"

"She's unforgettable, isn't she?"

"Does she owe you money?"

"Not me. I made sure never to work with her. I haven't heard anything about her since she left the neighborhood. I think she did well. You did some jobs for her, didn't you?"

"Yeah, she did well for herself. In the north, a wealthy neighborhood. I think she moved to Serrano or somewhere."

"I heard. She left her business here stinking to high heaven and resurfaced there smelling of roses. A butterfly emerging from a cocoon. But given the nature of the cocoon, I'd still have a healthy fear of the butterfly."

"Man, she didn't have many friends here when she left. She was getting death threats, so she called me. She was frightened for a time and . . . I had to . . . well, fortunately, the guy making the threats was an amateur. In the end I had to send my brother. I'd have gone myself, but it wasn't necessary. The guy never made another threat in his life."

"And you never worked with her again?"

"A year later, we recovered a bracelet or something that she'd left with her former partner."

"The one she bankrupted? Are you sure it didn't really belong to him?"

"At the time I didn't really think about it. But if it was his, he could have gone to the police. It wasn't like we stole it; I just played bodyguard. The man listened to reason. She paid well."

"Good businesspeople know they can cut corners on everything except their safety, especially when it comes to people like her."

"That was about . . . I don't know, eight years ago. Or more. I never heard from her again."

"Apparently, she has a proposal for me."

"That's strange . . . I don't know what to tell you. She always paid me without any trouble. If she's got where she is today, she can't have been cheating everyone all the time."

"That's why I'm going to see her. The work's dried up, Richard, and she knows it. I have to take what I can get. But a leopard can't change its spots. I just wanted to ask you because I knew that you'd done some work for her. Also, it means I can tell her that I came to see you . . . so she won't be tempted . . ."

He finished his cigarette. The smoke rose in blurry spirals, expanding and contracting to the hum of the fans, before dispersing into the thick, warm air of the courtyard. The machines dripped onto the worn, beat-up tiles.

The nicer part of town, an expansion driven by the nineteenth-century bourgeoisie and the Marquis of Salamanca, was reminiscent of the boulevards of Milan and every other European district built in the shadow of Haussmann's great Paris. Ever since Louis XIV, the French had known how to sell their ideal of urban planning to the rest of Europe.

This district, which was also just as exclusive as Milan, was brazen with its stone facades and expensive fixtures, a marked contrast from the brick and plaster of poorer areas. In just a few blocks, you could make the transition from traditional to aristocratic Madrid without even noticing: the narrow cobbled streets with their buried tramlines made way for imposing avenues and several lanes of traffic flanked by mansions, most of which had been converted into embassies and consulates, and reflective glass skyscrapers announcing the entry into the financial district. The back streets proudly displayed the stone architecture typical of the area along with the generous orthogonal layout, individual houses stretching hundreds of feet along the street with their own service entrances. Ladies in fur coats with severe gazes could still be seen wandering around as a reminder of the past.

In these surroundings, Jota stood out like a sore thumb, and he knew it. He'd been invited to move there in what felt like another lifetime, when he'd mingled with other wannabes, spoken like them, and drunk like them. And he hadn't enjoyed it at all. A lot of people wondered about that period: What might have happened if he'd continued his career as an art dealer and master forger? But that question, like all what-ifs, would never be answered, and Jota had never even asked it. He left that to others; it had lost all interest for him decades ago. Today, he'd intentionally chosen a scruffy, wrinkled shirt with a big stain on it and the low-slung pants that he only wore on special occasions, and this qualified as such.

He walked along the facades of the most exclusive hotels in the city, reflecting the disdain of the doormen back at them, past minimalist displays of major fashion firms frequented by the daughters of the men he had once been able to swindle. He checked the address on a wrinkled piece of paper and headed for a magnificent gate with a solid wooden door hidden to one side that stretched right to the ceiling. Its size was supposed to be indicative of the importance of the abode. Before entering the palace, he took a moment to light a cigarette.

Like the rest of the building, Morgades's office was large and well lit with balconies that looked out over the street, wooden shutters, and a stone balustrade. The thick floorboards, originals from the thirties, shook with every step, and you could feel the vibrations run up your leg, the real pleasure of proper floorboards that you only found in such places. Somber luxury and elegance oozed out of every feature, from the green-upholstered furniture and dark paintings to the smell of ancient wood. In her business, Morgades knew that you had to be impressive without showing off and to remind the nouveau riche, which formed the bulk of her clientele, that money was not necessarily power. When you entered her office, it wasn't to commission something—it was to request it. It was pathetic: they were so sure of themselves in their tailor-made but tasteless clothes, but they knew their place the moment they heard the creak of the floorboards, suddenly nervous on furniture their father's father never could have dreamed of, furniture that, as she would remind them, they could buy with their money but never truly possess. It just wasn't a part of their birthright.

Morgades may have spent her childhood in the poorest neighborhoods, but she had always belonged here. It was how she had been raised by her father, who had been from a great family fallen on hard times, and she'd made no apologies for doing whatever it took to return to where she belonged. Sometimes you must steal back what was once stolen from you. She appeared to have become an extension of her property: very blonde hair now white in places but strategically camouflaged without a hint of dye, designer sunglasses that may or may not have had prescription lenses, with which she cultivated a librarian-style look. She had severe, authoritarian features on a delicate face that might well have been beautiful; she was clearly attractive, but this was hidden behind a studied air, as though she were trying to be a kind of artistic housekeeper. It was a winning strategy. As Morgades had said to her friends on more than one occasion (but never to young women asking for advice), "A woman must know when her sexuality is a weapon and when it's a hindrance."

A young, impeccably dressed man with a distinctive speech affectation came to the door.

"Your appointment has arrived."

"Thank you. Offer him some coffee, and tell him to come in."

Jota walked straight in and slumped into a leather armchair with intentional clumsiness. Ignoring his rudeness, she got up to greet him in a very friendly manner.

"Jota, how lovely . . . it's such a pleasure to see you again, really it is. Have they offered you a coffee?"

"Yes, your lackey did. I said no."

"The same as ever, I see. Tell me—how are you doing? Still in the same business? I have so many questions. You have it in the blood, just like me: the best scout I've ever known."

Jota studied his rival, blank faced. It was just a negotiating pose, one of many possible approaches but one that always worked on the rich. Who was Morgades? What did she want of him?

"Thank you. But I don't remember ever having worked with you."

"Well, you never gave me the chance, which I found frustrating. I could never have dreamed to be in a position to give you a commission. But now, in contrast . . . now I'm working on another level."

"I see that you've done well for yourself."

"Many years of hard work and sacrifice."

"Whose sacrifice?"

Jota wasn't trying to insult her; it was part of a strategy. But when he looked into Morgades's eyes, he saw that they looked back just as intensely. He knew she was right: she was his equal. It would be hard to play her. This was someone who, as far as he knew, had never known the taste of defeat. Either that, or she had been able to conceal her failures very well, something he knew a little about too. So he allowed himself the luxury of being provocative, of playing the representative for all the losers in the neighborhood who hated her for being a successful woman, who called her a whore over and over again from the safety of their hovels, who accused her of having screwed them over, as she surely had. But wasn't it just that she'd gotten there first, before they did the same to her? At the end of the day, wasn't that what their business was all about? Morgades and he were just the smartest of the lot. In fact, he thought, Morgades was smarter: he may have flown higher at one time, but he'd crashed and burned while she'd ended up precisely where she wanted to be. So he decided to act the way she was expecting, to adopt the role she assumed he'd take and reveal his mistrust and discomfort, just to test her, to challenge her sense of diplomacy. He had nothing to lose. Besides, he understood her.

"I know that you don't believe me," Morgades said. "I know what you think of me, but it's not true. Nobody ever bothered to ask me for my version of events. I've worked hard to get where I am, and believe it or not, it's very important to me that you're here now. My father often talked about you, and I saw you when you went to the galleries with the dealers: Germans, Austrians . . . you were the one I expected to see in this neighborhood someday. My father was sure that was what fate had in store for you."

"The good times ended quite a while ago."

"I know that too. But you're still the only one I consider to be on my level."

And yet her face and body language said otherwise: her disappointment at his reaction, his predictable comments, how he was behaving like all the other idiots. Jota was pleased; he had Morgades just where he wanted her. She was starting to show her hand.

"I finally have a special commission to offer you. Something you can do for me. It's not a big job, but I think we should regard it as the initial contact for a longer-lasting relationship. I'd like to think we could work together in the future. It's something that I've promised myself ever since I started out."

"I don't work in these circles. I never enjoyed it."

"It's not your world; it's mine. You and I are the only ones who ever deserved to get out of that rat race of cheap collectors and secondhand bargains."

Who was Morgades? What did she want with him? She stopped just when she should have made her offer, withdrawing into a flurry of cheap flattery that was beginning to annoy him. Suddenly, Jota wasn't so sure he could read her after all.

"Listen," Jota said. "You think we're sitting down together right now, but that's not how it is. You haven't found me: you're fifteen years too late."

"Wait—you haven't even let me begin. I'm not talking about art. It has nothing to do with that. In fact, it's what you do now. Just look at this, at least."

Finally, Morgades took some photographs from a drawer in her desk. Jota looked through them without lingering on any. They didn't do anything for him. He kept going through them, trying to find some meaning, to work out what he might be missing, but these were nothing but a succession of objects in display cases in a house: a porcelain sailor figure, a candlestick, a clock. All of them were ordinary, of questionable taste and little value. For a moment he was genuinely disconcerted, as though he were the victim of a prank.

"What's this?"

"It's a personal collection."

Jota's face broke into a sardonic smile.

"A collection . . ."

"I know—almost all of it is junk, but it holds emotional value for the client."

"Not almost all. The whole lot."

"Don't be so negative. Look at the lamp. It might be a Lalique, don't you think?"

Jota looked at Morgades, who remained humorless. A mask that only a few moments before he'd thought he could read had led him into an absurd situation. He felt completely off balance; he had no idea what this woman was playing at.

"It's a piece of shit, like all the rest of it. You summoned me here to look at these photos?"

"Tell me which you think is the most valuable."

"None of it."

"If you won't help me, then we won't get anywhere."

"They look like the kind of wedding gift you throw away the next day."

"Give me a price."

Finally, a straight question, but not at the time or in the way he had expected. Maybe Morgades didn't know how to deal with this either, or maybe she was messing with him. Maybe the only reason behind this whole charade was to show him what he already knew: that this commission was ridiculous. Was she trying to humiliate him? Was it bait? Was she expecting him to refuse this job so she could offer him the real one, only with him now in the position of having to beg? Jota recalibrated his thoughts; you couldn't negotiate when you didn't know what you were negotiating for. He reminded himself of his initial position: he had nothing to lose coming here, but he wasn't going to ask for anything.

"I don't know why you asked me here, but we've wasted enough time already." The chair creaked as he stood up.

"Wait. My client thinks it's all worth the same, but you need to price something. Tell me how much the clock is worth."

Morgades picked a photograph from out of the group: a clock on a gold pedestal, not awful but hardly indicative of great taste. Without looking at the photo, Jota studied Morgades again, unable to read her expression. Jota still didn't know what to say.

"I can't value a photo just like that. Do you know how this works? Not like this, at least not between professionals."

"You know as much as I do; you don't need any more information: the clock would seem to be the most valuable piece. It was made in Spain before the war."

"The First World War, you mean. It's a cheap copy of French models, faux symbolist. It must be from before 1912, 1910. You mentioned Lalique, but these people would never have heard of him."

"Now give me a price."

Jota reacted immediately. He refused to play along.

"You can't get a clock like this for less than three thousand."

"You know it's not worth a thousand. But it doesn't matter; you don't understand. I don't want a clock like that one. I want that clock."

Jota was silent for a moment. He looked incredulously at the photograph and then back at Morgades.

"What? This one?"

His question was met with silence. He was confused. He scrutinized Morgades's face again and realized that this might really be it. It might be the actual reason she'd called him. Morgades might not be playing with him, or if she was, it was by giving him an impossible commission. Whether it was worth one or three thousand euros, it was a commission no one would take. He grew even more incredulous.

"That's impossible."

"Why? You don't think it's an interesting commission? You think I would call you here to buy a thousand-euro clock? You're the only one who can find what I'm looking for."

"I think this is bullshit. You might as well light a candle and make a wish. You can use that candlestick behind you—it's from a church. Made between 1800 and 1830, if I'm not mistaken."

"Yes, you're very smart, but you don't know everything. The clock was sold along with the rest of the lot in Madrid less than five years ago. It came from a family that had fallen on hard times and was forced to sell off all their things. That's all I know. I'm pretty sure that if we find one of the pieces, we'll find the rest, and that's what my client wants. So that's what we have to go on. If anyone can find that clock, it's you. And there's plenty more work where that came from. You have no idea what people are willing to pay to get back objects from their past. This is a niche no one is exploiting, and we could corner it between us. You'll be able to forget about everything else, the secondhand stores, the shitty little searches. If we do this job well, it'll be good times all over again."

Jota leaned back in his chair, still dubious but on firmer ground. So this was a real job. *A "small" commission*, he said to himself, a shitty lot but something they could search for based on concrete information. Morgades had played her cards well. He didn't know whether to show interest or laugh in her face. He studied the impassive woman. Who was Morgades? Suddenly he realized with a shiver that this was how her former partners must have felt. He looked at the photograph again and tapped it with his finger as he tried to decide what to do. Should he stick his head into the lion's mouth and name a price? He took out a cigarette, and Morgades passed him a silver ashtray without a word. After inhaling deeply, he spoke again.

"Maybe . . . but all the pieces are very ordinary. None of them are unique. It'll be hard to differentiate."

"Look at this." She showed him a close-up of the side of the clock, which had a blurry mark on it.

"A maker's mark?"

"Yes."

"I don't recognize it. It must be a very small manufacturer. A jeweler maybe. Of course, it's not . . . none of the big ones. Is the corona twenty-two centimeters?"

"Eighteen."

"And you don't have any more information or a better photo?"

"Yes, I have more photographs. I see that I've piqued your interest."

"So?"

"I want you to find it. Don't try to fool me. It's crucial for our business that you find the original. If you get caught trying to fake it, we wouldn't just miss out on future opportunities, but you'd be putting me in a very compromising position. It's nothing personal, but I hope we understand one another. I won't give you what you need to make a forgery. I could do that myself. There can't be many clocks in that model with that mark. The fact that you know it has one is enough. I'll know it when I see it, and so will you."

Just then, Jota smiled for the first time. Finally, the whole picture. He realized that Morgades had been leading him on from the start, making him curious about a commission he'd never have accepted initially. *This woman really is good*, he said to himself. He started to come up with a new plan, but he needed more information.

"You're pretty difficult, aren't you? Did it work? Should it work?"

"It doesn't matter."

So that was how it was: he was hooked, and she was keeping her cool because money was no object, and she was trying to keep that fact from him. Hence the roundabout way they'd come to it. Hence her direct questions. How much was this harpy making out of this this deal? Jota, a wily old dog himself, opted for an absurd price.

"Ten thousand, no invoices, no papers. I pay enough taxes already."

"What? That's daylight robbery!"

"You know very well why you called me. And you were right—I like the project. Ten thousand, and you'll get the clock. The other pieces aren't part of the deal."

"The right price is the first one you mentioned: three thousand. I can't offer you any more."

"You called me here for a three-thousand-euro job? You find someone who'll do it for three thousand, and if you ever find the clock, I'll buy you both dinner. I can give you some names if you like."

"I can't go higher than four."

Now that he had all the information, Jota decided on a move that could well cost him the job. He stubbed out his cigarette and headed for the door.

"Six thousand! That's the most I'm allowed. I can't go any higher, I swear."

Jota stopped.

"Six thousand euros for a clock you could get at auction for . . . your client is pretty damn committed. Tell them it's eight. If they are willing to pay six, they'll pay eight. I could give a shit about your cut. Two thousand in advance, the rest on delivery. If I don't find it, the two thousand will cover my expenses. Call me to confirm, or find someone else."

"If you're making me deal with all that, I want more: if you find the clock, I want to meet the seller. It's essential that we confirm the source—we'll use them as our certificate of authenticity."

"Yes, and it'll help you find the other pieces. What if I can't give you a name?"

"Then the deal's off, and I'll consider myself cheated."

"I'll take the photographs."

"Here are the JPEGs."

Morgades held out a small USB drive. Jota took it and inspected it for a moment as though it were an alien artifact. Then he dropped it dismissively on the table and turned around.

"Better give me the photos."

Back in his neighborhood, Jota walked through the seedy park where teenagers had gathered ever since he was a child. It was just a square of grass with a few bushes and trees separated by decorative wrought-iron railings, some sandy paths, and benches that were always occupied by said kids. But now they were dealers in their thirties, still living with their parents, waiting for potential buyers, listlessly conversing about their empty lives. Recognizing him, they said hello as he passed by. Farther on, where students tended to sit in circles smoking joints, they thought him just another loser from the neighborhood. A young girl disinterestedly kissing her boyfriend looked up as he went by and leaned away from her lover for a moment. He reacted timidly, afraid that he'd upset her.

"Laura? Is something wrong?"

"What? No, I just don't want to anymore."

While the boy fretted, Laura's honey irises, which had strange black dots right under the pupils, a feature her friends called her "second eyes," followed Jota curiously. She remembered him. She felt an impulse to shout out and explain who she was, but the words never left her mouth. Laura may have intimidated her boyfriends with her unpredictable behavior, but she had her own inhibitions. She stared at Jota like he was an enigma that somehow affected her.

Jota had stopped to talk to a man of about his age but who had a far ghostlier air: a junkie, one of the few from his generation still standing. The man had been scaring children for twenty years; he was a nobody beholden to an addiction he claimed to have beaten. They arranged to meet later at a friend's store so he could show Jota his wares: junk and stolen goods. He barely looked human, but people still called him Raulito, a diminutive that may once have been affectionate, had soon become disparaging, and now meant nothing at all. Raul had been one of the smart kids, top of his class. He'd savored life and sampled everything it had to offer until, still young, he'd gone too far. Now he simply served as a reminder of a lost generation. He scratched out a living doing odd jobs for guys like Jota and Adolfo, living with his ancient mother, who was able to rest easy now that he was with her again. The moment he assured her that he'd beaten his addiction, she forgot all about everything he'd stolen from her, all the damage he'd done.

Jota was growing bored waiting in the car parked on Calle Suelta. He threw another cigarette butt out the window and realized that a pile had formed on the asphalt. *I must stink of tobacco*, he said to himself, but still he delved back into the pack, which was now almost empty. Just then, Miriam came out of the building where she worked. He honked his horn a couple of times, but she didn't notice and headed in the opposite direction, toward the metro station. Jota leaned out of the window and shouted her name.

She turned around, frightened until she caught sight of him. He clearly saw her face crinkle in disgust before rearranging itself into formal politeness, a careful smile that he returned as he waved. She pointed to the metro and waved goodbye.

"No! I came—" But she didn't give him a chance to explain himself. He got back into the car and started it, swearing to himself. *Fuck!* Where had their relationship gone so wrong? How many years had it been since he could talk properly to Miriam? He remembered the girl who stared at everything wide eyed, like a camera that registered everything around her. A sweet little miracle who found something special in every moment, who listened to him breathlessly. He caught up with this unrecognizable woman.

"Hello, Jota. What a coincidence. But you needn't have come all this way. I'm going to take the metro, and you'll lose your spot."

"Hello, Miriam. You're looking very nice."

"Thank you."

"Why take the metro? I'll give you a lift home—it's on my way."

"Thank you, but I'd rather take the metro. I have to do some shopping. I'll get off in the center."

"Fine by me. I'll go with you. I haven't seen you in a while—we can catch up."

She glared at him in frustration. "Catch up? Since when do you care about doing that?"

"I've always cared. Come on; get in the car."

"No, Jota, I'm taking the metro. I have nothing to say to you."

"I think you do."

"You think you have something to say to me? What about Adolfo? Why don't you talk to him? You men, incapable of talking about your problems. What's wrong? Is your friend depressed? Well, why doesn't he talk it over with me? I am his wife, after all. This has nothing to do with you."

"It's not that."

"Yes, it is. You're worried because you think he's in trouble. But when I'm in trouble, Jota doesn't come along asking what's wrong."

"I've been meaning to talk to you for a while . . ."

"Talk about what? You don't talk, Jota—you just sit and listen so you can judge people in silence. It used to hurt—for years it hurt—but now I don't care anymore."

"Why don't you get in the car?"

"Because I don't need to answer your questions. I'm not seeing anyone, Jota. I'm not cheating on your little friend, even if it is the least he deserves. All that's over, OK?"

"Miriam."

"I'm not seeing anyone. I told you."

"I didn't ask that."

"You don't have to. I know what you're thinking." Miriam, the excited little girl so in love with all the wonders the world had to offer. Miriam, whom he'd lost many years ago, who had become a stranger to him. "Have you been a saint with all your girlfriends? Why did Pilar leave you? What about Rocio? Didn't they get sick of your disappearances, your cheating?"

"I didn't come to talk about my life. There's nothing to say."

"And yet you judge mine. But I know all about your life. Too fucking much."

"You never met any of them. And we weren't married."

"Only because you didn't have the balls. Because none of them was Laura, that's why."

"I did everything I could for you. And all I'm asking is that you don't hurt your husband."

"Yes, you did a lot. You practically raised me. That was thirty years ago, and you still think I belong to you. But I don't. I married your best friend and had his kids, and now I have to put up with his depression. And the boredom. You could have saved me from this shitty neighborhood, but no, I stayed, and when you vanished, I was left here eating shit with your ex-partner and all the business you left up in the air. I'm the one who keeps the household going and pays for the girls' school, so don't come lecturing me about my private life as though I were still a naive twenty-year-old. Now I'm the one telling you to grow up, telling your friends to grow up instead of living on memories of a long-dead world. I'm a woman, and I need to feel alive. Do you know what that is? Because I haven't felt it for a long time. I've missed Jota for years, just like I miss David. But you know what? At least he's dead—he's really, truly gone. You may never have turned the page, but you're just as dead. You're still wallowing in your shit and your memories. Let me live my grown-up life. I've earned it."

Miriam headed for the metro without giving him a chance to follow her, not that he would. She'd said it all. When had he lost her? She had been as harsh as she could be. In her frustration she'd stirred up as much shit as she could, all dredged up from the bitterness of her life. He knew that it was his fault that he'd lost her, the girl who'd thought everything was magical. The girl who had somehow disappeared.

Jota closed his eyes, and for the first time in a long time, he saw the flames rising. He could feel the heat of the fire. He opened them again, unsettled. He sensed something; he had a strange feeling that everything might be about to change, for better or worse. Jota didn't know if he was ready. Maybe this time it really would be the end of him. The flames were growing taller.

Again, the hunters were waiting in the night.

Cars drove along the main roads; in the distance voices could be heard, heated arguments and shouts for joy. A group of people had gathered in an alley trying to decide where the party should go next. They disappeared. The narrow streets were silent and intimidating in the orange light of the old lamps.

The man looked back to where the group had been and told himself that he hadn't seen them, that it was just a coincidence. Maybe he could shout for help and find refuge in the crowd or somewhere to hide. But they'd hear him first. And then the police would come, and he didn't want that.

He scoured his memory again, trying to get his thoughts in order. He was thinking objectively, without a trace of feeling: no one else had been in the house. And they'd only left dead bodies behind. There was no doubt about that: the bloody scene, the dead woman on the bed . . . he went through each detail in turn, trying to make sure he hadn't overlooked anything. No one else had been there; they hadn't left any witnesses. He was sure of that.

Then his eye began to throb with intense pain. He couldn't see, but he knew that it must be bleeding. He touched his sunglasses as though he could feel the wound behind them. Now he heard more footsteps and a low whistle along with a stifled laugh. It was their calling card. They were letting him know they were there.

They hadn't found him yet, but they were close. They were trying to goad him into showing himself, but if he stayed where he was, it would only be a matter of time. Escape was his only hope: he'd done it before; he could do it again. He wanted to get out to a plaza, mingle with the tourists, find the police, and ask for help. When you were doing something violent, you could suppress your emotions and act automatically, but when you were afraid, it was the fear that controlled you. Adrenaline made you hesitant, got your heart pumping, froze your mind, and forced you to act instinctively. It was a useful evolutionary response when you were trying to flee from immediate danger but could get you making bad decisions when you were facing a calculating enemy. He ran toward the light. As he went, he listened for footsteps behind him, and when he didn't hear any, he felt safe for a moment. A large, well-populated street stretched out before him. He got ready to call for help, but his voice failed him. A pair of shadows appeared in front of him; one of them blew that low whistle and stifled a giggle. Before he could react, someone came up to him from behind and caught him by the ankles. He fell forward. The man who'd knocked him down kneed him in the back and quickly moved to pin his arms as he struggled to get free. A second man grabbed him by the hair and pulled his head back like a trussed calf. The man tried to shout out, but the third shadow cut him off with a kick to the neck. He heard a voice behind him talking with a fourth figure he hadn't seen. The speaker was filming something with a camera.

"Are you done—did you get it?" The voice sounded nervous. "They want it recorded. Are you sure? Don't fuck with me."

"Shut up." The blond man turned back to him. "This is your last chance. Who hired you? Who was part of your team? If you talk, we'll let you go."

Their prisoner, ordinarily a tough, grizzled man, started to cry like a small child.

"That's all I know—I swear. It was set up by a guy called Xavi. He was the one who made contact with us. He called my partner, and we never saw him again. That's all I know. I can't . . ."

"Your friend died like a dog. And so will you."

There couldn't have been anyone in the house when they'd gotten there. They'd disabled the security system without any trouble and moved quickly. He had been alerted by a muffled sound; someone had been shuffling around in their sleep. Someone who wouldn't be alive much longer. He and his partner, hungry for action after their dose of speed, had exchanged fleeting looks and known that the time was right. They'd been determined to find an outlet for their pent-up energy, unaware that it would end with a pool of blood around the bed, the bodies, the noise, the screams, the others coming up. If he'd known that then, he wanted to say, he wouldn't have done it. But nothing he had to say would have made a difference. The man, pleading as he sobbed, realized that it was all over, but he didn't even have the wherewithal to ask them to make it quick. All he felt was fear. Oh, God, he didn't want to die—he didn't want to die now. All he could see was darkness, and the whistling shadow didn't give him any more time to think. The shadow slit the man's throat with a knife, like a cow's in a slaughterhouse. There was a muffled scream and a splash of blood while a white liquid began to flow from his nose and bubbles emerged from his mouth. A fraction of a second later, his head fell. The young man who was holding him let him go.

"Fucking hell, that's disgusting! But didn't they want us to film it?"

"Who cares? It's done."

They hurried off into the night, leaving the body lying in a puddle of its own blood.

2

Raul, the middle-aged junkie, came to the antiques shop where Jota and his partner did their deals. He exuded the submissiveness that addicts learned to adopt, like mistreated dogs, the result of a life in which you must beg to survive. He was carrying an old backpack from which he took a large, tattered plastic supermarket bag, its contents poking through holes. Adolfo spread the objects across the counter and quickly evaluated them: a brass ashtray, a nickel picture frame, a candlestick, an imitation Lladró pastoral figure of a teenage girl with a hole in the crotch and a penis drawn in marker. With disgust he crammed it all back into the bag before turning to Raulito, annoyance etched all over his face.

"Fuck, that's disgusting. It's all junk."

He only took a couple of pieces, paying a few coins for each. After Raulito had left, he turned to Jota.

"The iron cross guy wrote again. What do you think?"

"Forget it. I'm going to do the deal with Morgades. She has a good idea. I think it'll work. She might be an untrustworthy old bitch, but she's smart. Look," Jota said, handing over the photograph of the clock. "A client is looking for this piece and a whole lot along with it. It might be junk, but who cares what they want it for? If I do this job well, there might be more personal commissions to come. I'd be working for wealthy clients again."

"I thought you gave up on that market a long time ago."

"This is different," Jota was surprised to hear himself reply. He knew it wasn't. Had he sunk so low that he needed those clients again? Perhaps. "These aren't aficionados. Look at it."

His partner looked at the photo properly for the first time.

"Fuck, this is worthless. I could understand if it was old, but it was made less than a hundred years ago. I've got five just like it somewhere. Why are you working on shit like this? I can't believe it. How much are you going to charge?"

"A lot."

"This can't be worth much."

"The deal isn't done, but I'm pretty sure they'll agree. If not, she wouldn't have called me."

"You didn't say how much."

"Four thousand."

"Four thousand! Four thousand euros? That can't be right—either this woman's crazy, or it's some kind of scam. She's going to fuck you over. You're making a mistake. There's something fishy going on."

Jota was flustered for a moment. He lit another cigarette and turned to his partner seemingly to explain himself, but really he was thinking out loud.

"It's not a scam. It's an odd commission. They're not looking for that model of clock or something by the same maker; they're looking for that exact clock. It might be worthless, but it has to be that one." He smiled at a thought he didn't share with his partner. He was relishing his plan. "It's like a collector's market for unique pieces, but these don't have any real value. We won't have any competition, and we'll avoid the same old rackets. Think of the profits. How many rich people out there are looking for unique but worthless pieces?"

"I don't know, but if they haven't found it yet, it's because it's impossible to find. Can you hear yourself? Now I think you're the one who's gone crazy."

"Why would someone want to find something that isn't worth anything? For sentimental reasons, family . . . whatever you like. It doesn't matter. How would you lose something like this? Burglary, pawned when you're down on your luck. There aren't many other options. This is our world. If we can't find it, no one will."

"Then no one will, probably."

Jota smoked and found himself in the grip of a long-forgotten memory: Adolfo despairing of his ideas, trying to control him while he and David ran around enjoying themselves, ready for anything. Where had David gone? Where was his memory? Jota saw a hint of a mirage, the excitement of the chase, and although he knew he was kidding himself, for a moment he felt alive again. And maybe that was the real reason he'd taken the job; maybe he should thank Morgades for shaking him out of his lethargy. In the darkness, the flames died down, receding in his memory.

"Look at the photograph. There's a maker's mark here. I never said I'd find that specific clock, but if I can't find one exactly like it, then I've been wasting my time all these years."

"But you can hardly see anything. Don't you have a better image?"

"Of course not. Morgades isn't stupid—she's not going to give me too much help. She thinks she's got me where she wants me. This way she doesn't think I'll be able to fake it."

"A red rag to a bull."

"For the money she's paying, I'm happy to charge off wherever she likes."

"Hmmm . . . if it's such a hard job, such a strange commission . . . are you sure that's what you're charging? If these people are as rich and desperate as you say, you could have asked for more."

"Don't be so suspicious. There'll be time for that. We need to get a foothold in the market first. Then we'll raise the price."

"So what's my cut?"

"That depends on how much help you are. To start with, all I know is that it was sold as part of a worthless lot five years ago. It must have gone to an antiques place somewhere; that's where we need to begin."

"And my help consists of finding out who the hell sold it, while you do the legwork."

"Exactly. If we track down the original seller, we're home free. We just need to introduce them to Morgades as a guarantee and make up a story about how we got it back. And if by chance we find the real one, then your percentage will go up. The amount I'll save by not having to make it."

"That's a pipe dream."

"Think of the money to be made, and open your mind a little. You could use it."

Secretly, even Adolfo was happy to have a new job; a little fresh air had blown into his stagnant world.

The yellow sign for the Castillo de Loarre was still three-quarters lit, while the other section was the depressing orange of burnt-out neon, just like last year. But the owner never found time to change it. In fact, he never even considered it: Who had time to think of things like that when you opened up at seven every morning and closed at one at night? "Hotel management isn't a life—it's a sentence," he told his son as often as he could, but all the boy could see was an aging loser with a ridiculous moustache, his fingers stained dark with tobacco, his back bent with responsibility, and his gaze weak with exhaustion. He, meanwhile, was still selling drugs in the clubs, making more money than his father had ever seen. The old man was a nobody who didn't understand what life was all about.

The Castillo de Loarre had seen better times, but it was still where people of Jota's generation met up, and anything that happened in the neighborhood was still discussed there; information was still passed from mouth to mouth, although that was slowly changing. The large bar still had its aluminum surface from the eighties and now attracted young hipsters ready to repeat the mistakes of their parents, even if they did claim to be doing it ironically. A set of partially laid tables and chairs gave the place a scruffy air, as though things only kept moving out of inertia, but the energy was slowly fading away.

At the table closest to the door, four of Jota's friends were playing cards, just like they did every afternoon, accompanied by a pair of onlookers who came and went, sometimes sitting in for one player or another. Once Jota had completed the customary round of greetings, he waited for Mariano, the owner, to pour him a gin and tonic, a drink that was fashionable now but just ten years ago had been seen as stuffy. It had always been his drink. He paid no attention to passing fads, although it was very possible that he'd started drinking them as a teenager because of one. But that was back when he didn't drink every day. It had been years since he cared what other people were drinking, and he was utterly contemptuous of the kids arguing over whether lemon or cucumber was better or the best brand of tonic water. He asked for change for a twenty, went over to a machine hidden in a corner, and started to shove coin after coin into it. When one of the cardplayers got up to leave, they invited him to join them, but he declined with a half smile.

"Come on, Jota—you know you want to."

"No, Rodrigo, you're all addicted to that game."

"But you never play anymore."

"It's just that gambling—"

"The other day, Mari Cruz was asking after you. Why don't you come round for dinner on Saturday?"

Just then, Jota's phone started to ring. "Sorry . . . hello?"

"Hello, Jota, it's Clara Morgades. I've just spoken to the client. It wasn't easy, but in the end he agreed to your terms."

"Fine, I'll pass by tomorrow for the advance, and you can give me all the information you have."

"It's a pleasure to be working with you."

"Let's hope so. I'll set things in motion."

He hung up. Morgades had done it. She really had played her cards well; she must be desperate. And she'd managed to keep what was a ridiculous deal just within the bounds of sanity. Eight thousand euros, off the books, and more might just be around the corner. Jota was satisfied. Eight thousand euros for a job that shouldn't last longer than a couple of months and that might lead to much more. He hadn't had a commission like that for years. Morgades had gotten what she wanted, but he'd gotten more. He turned back to the man he had been talking to.

"You know what, Rodrigo? I'm going to take you out for lunch."

The almond trees were blooming early, their pink-and-white blossoms pale and cold in the cool air, which would last for about another month. Jota lifted his coat collar and stepped up his pace to stave off the freezing morning. He headed for a large store near the Plaza de la Independencia, on the edge of Morgades's neighborhood, just over a mile from her office. The shop window loomed large and dark under a patrician sign that read VELÁZQUEZ ART GALLERY AND AUCTION HOUSE, a reference to this part of the city. This was one of the main hubs for antiques and collectors in the capital, maybe the most important. Over six thousand square feet of display cases with several armed guards stationed discreetly in strategic locations. Through it circulated people who had just come to browse, the odd wealthy tourist, and people doing deals or asking about specific pieces at one of the different service counters. Jota went over to a salesman in a tie who greeted him familiarly.

"Good morning—how's it going?"

"Fine. Let's hope it lasts. I've come to see Pilar."

"Pilar is unavailable right now. Perhaps I can help you—"

"You can't, but if you let her know I'm here, that would be a great help."

"I know that you usually deal with her and that you've worked with us in the past, but now that the program is being implemented, she doesn't work with the general public. You know how it is with computers: they say that a new tool is going to make everything better, but I don't see how. Have you been to our website?"

"I'm looking for this." He held out the photo of the clock.

"I'm not familiar with the model. Is it French?"

"It's Spanish."

"Meneses?"

"No, an imitation. What I need to know is if you've ever had anything similar in."

"Similar? No, nothing similar."

"Huh, listen—do you go over everything that's auctioned here?"

"No, of course not. That would be impossible."

"So can you tell Pilar that I need to talk to her?"

The man made a face but realized that he was in an impossible situation. "Excuse me a moment."

He disappeared through a side door, and Jota waited. One of the security guards eyed him in a distinctly unfriendly manner, and he flashed him a goofy smile in return. Just then, the man reappeared.

"This way, please."

Jota followed him, still smiling at the guard.

The corridor was narrow and poorly lit. They passed by entrances into different warehouses until they got to a reinforced door, at which the man knocked. A woman's voice invited him in, and the man left Jota alone with a glance goodbye. Pilar's office looked like a storage cupboard: it was full of boxes, files, and different outdated models of computer arranged on various shelves, some of which looked suitable for auction themselves. They greeted each other informally, with the intimacy of old friends, in the knowledge that they wouldn't let each other down. It was as though they'd been a couple for years and all the love, resentment, and hatred were in the past, replaced by security and routine. After a brief conversation, Jota showed her the photograph of the clock, which she studied closely.

"You don't have a date, a reference, a jeweler, nothing? Look, I know you think that computers are magical contraptions, but they're just tools. If you can't give me any real information, we're not going to get anywhere."

"Your friend outside was right—with this marvelous new invention, nothing will escape you. I'll be obsolete."

"The boldness of ignorance. Hmmm . . . is something similar any good for you? Here, French clocks 1880 to 1900." She started to scroll down through a large catalog. "See this?"

"Yes, the heads are similar."

"It's a copy. That one's a symbolist copy too. So tacky. They were in fashion in the last decade of the nineteenth century, but they're still ugly. We sold that model for . . . seven hundred euros, two years ago. They aren't hard pieces to find; there are plenty around. Yours is rarer. It's not very nice because it mixes two different styles, both copied poorly."

"You don't think it's silver?"

"Yes, it's silver, but . . . are you sure that it wasn't made earlier?"

"Yes."

"Then it must be from a small town, somewhere provincial. In Madrid and Barcelona these had gone out of fashion by then."

"Yeah, they were copying other things."

"And they still are. It must be from the north."

"Are you sure?"

"We've sold a lot of Andalusian pieces. Silversmiths from the south are better in terms of quality, but they're always tainted by colonial rococo excess; they don't hold back. *Ad maiorem Dei gloriam.* You might find something like that in the Bay of Biscay but not elsewhere. In the north, they copied the European styles—the haute bourgeoisie went off to 'bathe' in the sea in France. They loved decadence. They had a lot of hang-ups."

"Will you do me a favor? Can you copy this photo onto the computer, and if you sell a similar-looking piece, let me know?"

"You want to restore it?"

"If I can find it."

"What if a similar model comes in?"

"If that was likely, you'd have said already. Let me know, but seven hundred euros is a lot for a clock like that."

"Fine. I'll let you know if I find something that might help you."

Jota left the warmth of familiar surroundings and headed back out onto the cold street. He crossed the city again and went into the poorer neighborhoods, an old town that had slowly been absorbed by the capital as it grew, losing its identity but maintaining some of its rural features: the one- or two-story houses and a calm atmosphere that contrasted with the roar of the center. The area tended to be eulogized by old people who remembered how it used to be when they were young, another life before modernity and all the drugs and alienation that came with it changed their offspring's lives forever.

He found an extremely narrow street and went into a store that, with the blind pulled down over the door, looked abandoned at first sight. It was a store for timepieces. Its walls were toasted cream, an anachronism left over from the postwar period. The wallpaper had long since begun to flake in concentric rings of damp. Hunched over a small easel with barely any light was an old man well past retirement age working on an exquisite-looking mechanism. He greeted Jota affectionately and listened hard as Jota explained about the clock. Everything the man did, he did in a slow, calculated fashion.

"So . . . you say this is a maker's mark?"

"Yes. As I said, you can barely make it out, so don't bother."

Jota repeated everything several times with unusual patience. This man had already been old when he was still a child, sitting in his dusty store, oblivious to the world, trapped in his own dimension of motions and precision clockwork. Once—Jota couldn't remember when, but he was still very young—on one of the few occasions when they'd met in a bar, the man, forever stuck in his own world, had said to him, "Did you know that Einstein said that if he hadn't been a physicist, he'd have been a watchmaker?" Jota the teenager had been impressed. "Einstein, absolutely," the man had said, chuckling to himself with the same candor with which he accepted jobs today. "Einstein knew what he was about. He may have deciphered time, but we have to organize it. My boy: mine is a very special trade." Ever since, Jota couldn't see the old man without also thinking of the famous image of the physicist sticking out his tongue. The idols we encounter in our adolescence rarely go away. This man was an institution, at least to those who still remembered, who still understood what he did. One day, he'd dry up in his store like a husk among his artifacts. He was one of the few people whom Jota still respected.

"I'm too old for this kind of thing."

Jota sighed and summoned his patience. "I told you: what I want to do is find a case with the original mark on it and rebuild the rest completely. It doesn't look like it'll be too difficult."

"You won't be able to. It's all one piece, see? It looks like the work of a craftsman . . . if it's from 1900, you won't be able to solder it. Look at this line—you can't hide a soldered joint like that. If the buyer knows their stuff, you won't be able to fool them."

"You're always right, you old fossil."

"What I'd do . . . I think . . . if you can fool me . . . if you believe in it . . . then it's a good copy."

"Are you saying that we need the exact same clock?"

"Well, the same model. Or the front at least. Do you want a motion? A motion from that period would be quite expensive."

"I don't want one that tells the time, you crazy old man—I want a rusty old mechanism that will fit inside the case. No one will know the difference."

"So it doesn't have to work?"

"No, but it has to look as though it belongs."

"Ah, if it doesn't have to work, then it won't be so expensive."

"How much?"

"Uh . . . a hundred euros?"

"Sixty."

"Fine."

Jota laughed. "So you're going to give me some rusty old mechanism you've got hidden away back there, you old swindler. I always pay what you ask. A hundred euros. Do a good job, and I'll give you a hundred and fifty. How are things going otherwise?"

"Not well. I should have closed years ago. I get by on the work you give me. Rafael came by yesterday."

"Rafa's incompetent."

"He was when you met him, but now he's giving me a lot of jobs."

Rafael Sanz was a great scout, and Jota knew it. He knew it, and it hurt because he'd taught him everything he knew. But like anyone with the talent and willpower—and such people were in scant supply—Rafa had grown up and headed out on his own. He'd done something that Jota couldn't forgive even though he'd have done it himself, the same kind of thing he'd done at the beginning of his career. Jota had helped Rafa. Jota had been his mentor, and when he'd disappeared, Rafa had taken his place. What else was he going to do? Jota had lost five years, and when he came back, his strength and talent were gone. That became very clear in their circles. How had Rafa betrayed him when he was just taking what belonged to him by right? Still, Jota never forgave him because people could never forgive their own mistakes. Rafa represented his lost years, his fall from grace, the loss of his business and his rupture with his partner, whom Rafa had immediately begun to work with. He represented Jota's failure.

"For years he lived on my scraps. Everything he knows he learned from me. He must still be working with his faithful lapdog, Gabrielito. Rafael and Gabrielito, what a pair."

"But now he has a lot of jobs for me."

"Then keep on working with him if you like."

"Are you angry because he worked with Diego after you split?"

"That was a long time ago. Do you know what that hero Gabriel, Rafa's scout, did? He beat up Raul, the junkie that brings us things. You know, the one who lives with his mother. He beat up a wretch, a loser who can barely stand, claiming he'd stolen something. So that's the future of the profession. The next time I see Gabriel, I'm going to put him in his place so he never forgets who he is. It's not because of dusty old stories only you remember, old man."

"They're the ones that still move us."

"You, maybe."

"And you, Jota. You too."

"Don't be so sure. Rafa stopped working for Diego years ago too. It's not about that. I don't like him—I never did. Not him and not his assistant."

"These days he's doing a lot of imports. He's a customs agent. He brings a lot in from China."

"Perfect. The moment he finds someone to do your job in China, get ready: he'll ditch you without a second thought. That's how your friend Rafa works."

And with that, Jota brought the conversation to an end. He handed the old man the photograph.

"Here. I'll leave the photo with you so you have something to think about other than ancient history. Get to work; the crown is eighteen centimeters."

The old man carefully placed the photograph on a stand and looked at it for a little while. Then he smiled at Jota, a bright, childish smile. He took everything Jota had to say with good grace.

Jota was sitting in his parked car, once again lying in wait. This time, however, he was being discreet, hoping not to be seen. He was in luck. After a dozen cigarettes, he was rewarded. Just as he'd suspected, the telephone call had been right on. How could Miriam expect to keep something secret in this neighborhood? Especially from him? She came out the door of the seedy hotel where he'd been told she'd be, straightened out her clothes, listlessly looked each way, and walked casually to the nearest bus stop, unaware that Jota was watching her. It was a bitter sight for him to see her leaving the building like that. He felt bad for his friend but, although she'd never believe it, especially sorry for her. Jota didn't know when he'd lost her—perhaps he'd never know—but he felt the pain of knowing he'd failed someone, of seeing that she was unhappy. He could watch her, but he had no idea what to do next. What would he do with this information? Share it with Adolfo? No, it would destroy him. So what, then? Jota refused to admit it, but all he'd done was share in his friend's suffering and his sister's disappointment. Their shared frustration. He'd take responsibility—he didn't yet know for what. He'd live with the burden and decisions that had accumulated over time. Suddenly, he was hit by the kicker. The man left the hotel: he could have been anyone, but no, it was Gabriel, Rafa's assistant. Rafa might have been his rival, but at least he was a respectable scout. Gabriel, on the other hand, was a piece of shit, a good-for-nothing dealer who'd inveigled his way into the world of collectors, a bum. And now he was sleeping with Miriam and probably boasting about it to everyone.

Miriam had chosen to sleep with the guy who would humiliate her husband the most. But Jota wasn't going to do anything; he wasn't going to confront Gabriel or call Miriam. He had no intention of using the information he'd obtained. He had to let her live her life. Or ruin it. Jota was just going to deal with this betrayal little by little, the way you came to terms with a chronic disease. But Gabriel . . . Gabriel would pay. That he swore to himself.

As the days passed, Jota's workroom changed completely. He hung a corkboard on the wall and pinned different enlargements of the photo of the clock, highlighting specific details: some of them were underlined; others had sketches. A big enlargement showing the crown was life size at eighteen centimeters. Above that were other parts, also at 1:1 scale: both sides, the raised corners and contours, and several pages with separate parts. But the crown was at the center. The two tables began to fill up with clocks and parts, and they soon spread to a sideboard and, eventually, the floor. He'd put up a notice to remind the cleaning lady, who came by twice a week, not to touch his work area under any circumstances, as was usual when Jota was deep into a project.

Several weeks later, Adolfo called him excitedly with good news. For a moment, Jota forgot about the counterfeit and plunged back into the scouting work.

His partner awaited him triumphantly in the store like a schoolboy ready to correct his teacher's mistake.

"Once again, while you're busy building dollhouses, I'm finding leads. Don't you get tired of always being wrong?"

"I'd get tired if I didn't end up always having to do everything myself. Tell me what you've got, and I'll decide whether it's worth following up."

"In a few minutes, we're going to have to reconsider my cut. What do you want first: the good or bad news?"

"I don't know. You've never given me good news before."

"I know where your precious clock was sold. But that's the bad news too. Do you remember the African guy who used to work for Torres?"

Torres's name was poison to Jota's ears, and his friend knew it. Jota's annoyed grimace did not reveal just how much.

"A lot of Africans have worked for Torres."

"But this one, Abdelazil, and I go back some time. Until about three years ago, he made all the deliveries. Now he has his own van at the market. From the dates you gave me, I knew that if Torres had handled the clock, he'd probably be able to remember."

"Probably?"

"Definitely. He has a photographic memory. That's why Torres let him run the warehouse. You know he wouldn't give that job to just anyone. The African's a strange guy, but we get on well. He recognized the clock right away—the mixture of styles makes it memorable. Before I could say anything, he told me that he remembered it, that it came to Torres about five or six years ago along with a very cheap lot, and that fits with the information you gave me."

Jota thought for a moment before answering. Adolfo waited expectantly. He knew that the reaction wouldn't be good—not because the information was no good but because Torres was involved, and Jota didn't want to go down that path. *He might not want to*, Adolfo thought, *but sometimes you've gotta do what you've gotta do*, and he felt the naughty pleasure you felt when you annoyed the people you loved. Eventually, Jota spoke.

"And what's the good news?"

"Fuck, you don't believe me?"

"What proportion of antiques in Madrid does Torres handle? Maybe eighty percent? That's no revelation. What does your African expect now? For Torres to say, 'Yeah, we had it probably—who knows?' when I ask? 'Thank you, Abdewhatever, you were right?' How much did he charge for this wonderful information?"

"You've got the wrong idea. I did him a big favor a few years ago. He likes me. You don't charge for things like that; he's not getting anything out of this. I know that you don't like getting involved with Torres—no one does—but the information is genuine."

"I don't care about Torres. His foreman Fran still works there. He'll be more than willing to help me. That's not the problem. The problem is that it doesn't lead us anywhere, and the whole thing's getting out of hand. If other people find out that I'm looking for a piece, they might get in the way even if they have no idea what it's worth. They could screw up everything."

"Thank you for doubting my discretion. I know how to keep my mouth shut. If Torres sold it, his foreman will remember it. But there's more. Abdelazil recognized the order because it came from an old acquaintance: Diego, your former partner."

"Our old friend Diego."

"Yeah, but he's still speaking to me."

"No he isn't."

"Whatever. If my information is right, then I've given you the lot and the original owner—what more do you need?"

"For you to be right."

Adolfo saw what Jota was thinking: he was capable of ignoring the lead because of an old grudge. It was deeply annoying. *I'll go myself if I have to*, he thought. But they both went back a long way, so long that they always knew what was on each other's mind. It irritated them both to be read so easily.

"Are you going to Torres's warehouse?"

Jota looked as though he was about to answer but instead just stared back at his friend as he finished his cigarette. Then he clucked his tongue in resignation.

The industrial park was just under ten miles to the south, and the turn-off from the freeway wasn't well marked. Trucks came and went, slowing down the rest of the traffic. At the back of the lot were three warehouses, each signposted simply in basic lettering: **Furniture. Torres Antiques.** Delivery vans and one or two entrepreneurial cars were parked out in front. Although the wares were rarely available to the general public, you often found that the exhibition floor was full of people. The prices were tempting, especially for items that weren't earmarked for anywhere else, and you could get a good deal even if you weren't a professional.

Jota drove around the back and parked behind the third warehouse. An open door revealed its interior, which was full of large metal shelves of antique objects and pieces, like a huge junkyard. A couple of employees were unloading wardrobes from a van, some of them in pretty poor shape. To one side, a metal staircase rose up to a few small offices.

An employee came to meet him.

"Excuse me, the store is in the other building. This is a warehouse."

But he was interrupted by a voice. A man with a gaunt, pockmarked face and dry skin shoved his inferior out of the way so he could hug Jota.

"Shit, Jota!" Then he turned to the other man. "Run along—this man's a friend of the house. These new kids have no fucking idea. Of course, you never come by here, so they never get a chance to meet you."

"Hi, Fran. You're getting plump. Mari must be treating you well."

"And you're the same old bastard. What a surprise to find you here. How can I help you?"

"If you like, we can go for a quick beer, and I'll tell you."

"I can't right now; we're getting a delivery of a bargain lot. It's in a terrible state, and Torres chose today to come by. He's in my office in a shitty mood."

"Torres is here?"

"And this really isn't a good time."

"It doesn't matter. Look, I came to see if you can help me with something."

Fran and Jota spoke for a few minutes about the photo and the clock and the likelihood that it came through the warehouse.

"It has distinguishing characteristics. I suppose it might be possible to track it down, but it's not a very remarkable piece, not the kind you remember. Do you know whether we sold it ourselves or just kept it in the warehouse? You know that a lot of dealers rent space from us."

"I'm not sure—maybe it was in Diego Blanco's space."

"That's possible. We've held Diego's stuff in the past. Are you back in touch?"

"No, that's why I came to see you."

"But if it belonged to Diego, I can't help you. We don't keep the inventories of rental customers—we just give them the space."

"Maybe you sold his lot. I have more photographs to show you."

"Don't bother. I can't remember whether we ever sold Diego's lots, but I know that he's never brought in a clock . . ."

Jota wasn't listening anymore. He saw an obese man getting on in years observing him from the top of the staircase. He wore a light jacket and several gold necklaces and chains.

"Hello, Torres."

The figure didn't answer. The foreman stood back fearfully, knowing the trouble he was going to be in later for talking to Jota. But Jota paid no attention. He went up the stairs without being asked and followed the figure into the office, closing the door after him. He looked down at the warehouse below. Three foreign workers were sorting through the newly arrived stock. Fran reluctantly went back to work. Torres leaned back in his red leather chair. He looked like a power broker from the eighties. His tone was chilly.

"I hope you've brought my money."

"You're getting boring, Torres. You're always saying the same thing, but you live in cloud-cuckoo-land. You're the one who owes me. If I ever owed anyone, it wasn't you, and I paid for it for five years."

"Well, if you haven't come to pay me, what the hell are you doing here?"

Jota calmly reached into his jacket pocket and took out his pack of cigarettes. He lit up without offering one to Torres, who stayed quiet. Then he showed him the photo of the clock. "Recognize it?"

Torres scrutinized him far more closely than the photo.

"Huh . . . I know what you're looking for, and I have something that might interest you. It's funny, isn't it? A few years ago it was the other way around. I like that you've come here looking for help."

Jota didn't answer; he just continued to smoke.

"It's such a shame to see you running worthless errands. But I can give you a whole lot like this, including a candelabrum. You have the choice of five, seven, or nine arms; an ashtray; and a serving tray."

"I just want this clock. I know you bought it from an Andalusian family a few years ago. I need the name of the buyer, if you keep records."

"Did Fran tell you that?"

"He can't remember. I had the information already."

"Hmm . . . let me see. Yes, I think I remember something. Leave the photograph with me, and I'll find it for you. How much are they paying you for this?"

Jota gave him the archest look he could muster. He peered down at Torres like an entomologist studying an insect. An unpleasant, chubby insect he'd once worked for—or whose hand he'd once held, to be more accurate. Who always gave him the biggest commissions without quibbling over the price.

"You're the same fat old liar as ever. You wouldn't find it if you were sitting right on top of it."

"What the hell?"

"You've never seen that clock in your life. And you didn't buy it from a family. I was testing you."

"Who the hell do you think you are to come here and insult me like this?"

Jota put out his cigarette and got up without saying goodbye, ignoring Torres's shouts.

"How can a nobody like you have the gall to disrespect someone like me?"

Jota walked down the stairs. Torres followed him out of the office, waited until he'd gone a fair way down, and shouted to his employees, "Take a good look at him! The man you see before you could have been the best antiques dealer in the fucking country, and look where he is now! Remember his face, and make sure you never end up like him, you fools!"

But Jota was unmoved. He headed out of the building. Torres watched until he was sure that he'd gone and shouted some more to unburden himself of the rage that had been building up inside of him.

"He killed his best friend! That's what happened to him!"

The young men working on the ground looked up nervously, and a little curiously, for the first time. But Torres didn't return their gaze; his was still fixed on the door Jota had exited through. For a second he thought that Jota had heard him and was coming back, and he stumbled backward, pale faced. He knew he'd gone too far. *Always the bigmouth*, he thought, and now he almost wanted Jota to come back so he could explain himself or make some kind of an excuse. His throat was dry, and he knew that in thirty seconds he wouldn't be able to say a word. Torres remembered the Jota of twenty years ago, with dried blood on his hands and a recent scar he'd never seen but knew was there. A glassy gaze concealing an unquenchable rage. Torres remembered the image from his past and trembled like a leaf at the prospect of being confronted by the Jota who had left him high and dry. The Jota he was terrified of. His puzzled employees stared up at their boss's frozen expression and shaky hand. Then they looked toward the door, wondering if the man was indeed going to come back and why he had that effect on their boss, *the* boss, a fat, pompous, ridiculous man who until this day had never cowered before anyone. But there was only the sound of the car pulling away to join the rumble of the freeway. The employees got back to work, and Torres went back into his office, wondering what had driven him to shout like that, about how the past lurked in your mind and popped up just when it could do the most damage. *You killed your best friend, and nothing will ever change that.*

The owner of the bar was waiting at the appointed time, and although he was in his own establishment, his fear was making him sweat more than he'd have liked. His body was refusing to obey his instructions, broadcasting its own updates about the state he was in. His shirt was soaked through, like he'd just stepped out of the sauna, and his hair was plastered to his skull as though after a rain shower. His two sons were there to provide moral support, squeezing his shoulders to show that they'd stand firm with him, but the more they tried to help, the more panicky he felt: he'd lived a long life, but they were still young and had no idea what they were up against.

Finally, the moment came. The blond man appeared with unnerving punctuality, accompanied by three other men. The leader unceremoniously strode into the bar and sat down while his companions closed the shutters. He sat for almost two minutes without saying a word until the owner timidly opened his mouth to break a silence that was beginning to feel like a bad omen.

"I-I know your friends. They'll tell you about me. I'm reliable and loyal, I'm . . . I'm . . ."

"Then you'll know what I'm about to ask. I don't want to waste any more time than I have to. Who's Xavi?"

"I know, they said. But I don't know who he is. I never worked for him. I-I . . . I asked, but he's not from around here. It was a one-off thing."

"Who put you in contact with them?"

The owner gulped and felt the sweat running down his cheeks. It gathered on his moustache. His boys tensed up and tried to project strength, but the blond man ignored them.

"Th-that was what I asked, bu-but the only one who dealt with that was the Russian. He was the one who made contact."

One of his sons butted in with the eagerness of someone trying to help without really knowing what was going on.

"He wasn't Russian. We spoke, but he never came here."

The blond man didn't need to do anything; the father pulled hard on his son's sleeve, and he shut up immediately. The blond man looked on impassively.

"My son is telling you the truth. The Russian got those jobs. He must have been the contact, but he died two years ago of stomach cancer. We didn't know him, really. I never knew what business they were involved in, what they did—I swear on my father's grave. I . . ."

The blond man continued to observe them in silence. He realized that he wasn't going to get any more out of them. Still without saying a word, he got up, making the sons jump back. The father tried to keep control of his emotions, but his eyes closed involuntarily, as though he were dead tired, another side effect of the stress. When he managed to get them back open, making it seem like a long blink, he felt the sweat running down from his eyebrows, flooding his eyes with an unpleasant salty sensation. Through the cloudy haze he saw the blond man, who was utterly indifferent to his terror, leave, flanked by his companions. When the owner of the bar heard the car doors close and the engine start up, he couldn't hold back any longer. He started to cry like a scared little boy, hugging his sons and kissing them all over their faces.

The blond man's face darkened as he got into the car.

The shadow waiting for him in the rear seat leaned forward. "Nothing?"

"He was telling the truth. The contact is dead."

"That saves us some trouble."

"And reduces our options. It's a dead end."

"Or maybe not. The real search starts now. Isn't that why you hired me?"

3

The days passed slowly, but the work progressed. Sitting at the workbench in his studio, Jota was inspecting an old clock with a wooden stand as he finished a cigarette. He shoved a screwdriver between the stand and the case and knocked it in farther with a hammer to pry it away. Then he picked up the stand, set the rest aside, and started trimming and sanding it. He did his work calmly, with relish. Then he compared what he'd done to the enlargements of the clock and an image in an old French catalog that looked very similar. He painted and sanded again and again. Hours later, he put it on a shelf, next to four others that were almost identical but for slight stylistic differences, all of which were newly painted.

At the Castillo de Loarre, Rodrigo the police captain was playing his regular game with the locals until one of them whispered something malicious into his ear. Rodrigo turned around uncomfortably and looked out the window. He saw a figure and snapped his fingers, as though he were calling a dog to him. Then he went back to his game, but the man, after hiding for a moment, had decided to stay where he was. The cardplayers and onlookers nudged the policeman again, pointing out that he was still there.

The owner of the bar went outside to see what was going on but came back in while Rodrigo grew irritated by his companions' needling.

"Is he still out there? If he stays any longer, I'm going to have to remind him just who Rodrigo Fernández is."

"No, it looks like he's gone."

One of them went outside to look until he found Raul the junkie trying to blend in among the parked cars on the opposite side of the street. The man jubilantly came back inside.

"Ha ha. He's still there, Rodrigo! He can't take his eyes off you."

"The dumb bastard has forgotten all the times I've arrested him. This time I'll have to make it truly memorable."

The bar owner tried unsuccessfully to calm him down.

"Rodrigo, easy now. He's not bothering anyone. I'm sure he means no harm."

"What have I told him, what? That I don't want to see him around here. I don't want that kind of scum on my street!"

The other cardplayers tried to rile him up some more.

"Yeah, you told him!"

"None of them come by here anymore."

"They must be beginning to lose respect for you."

"That's it."

Rodrigo stormed out of the bar while the cardplayers sat back to watch the show. Mariano looked at them angrily.

"You guys talk out of your asses sometimes. Antonio, watch the bar for a moment, will you?"

"Come on, Mariano. We're just messing around. That piece of shit is going to get it now."

Mariano left through the back door, crossed a tiny patio full of empty beer cases, and rapped on an old wooden door. It was opened by Richard, the gym owner, who took up the entire doorframe. Inside, the atmosphere was tense. Jota seemed to be doing a deal with several men who shied away when they saw the newcomer, quickly hiding their merchandise. One of them stood up aggressively. Jota calmed them down but looked at Mariano in surprise.

"Don't worry—it's just the owner of the bar. What's going on?"

"Jota, I'm sorry. I didn't want to bother you, but your idiot friend Raul has been hanging around, looking for you. I told him to come back later because you were busy, but the fool stayed, and now Rodrigo's getting involved. Those bastards he plays cards with have been fucking around with him, and now he's determined to teach the guy a lesson. He's going to take him down to the station. What's that idiot doing around here?"

"He must not know where to find me. I haven't been around much in the past few days. Can't you deal with Rodrigo?"

Mariano shook his head. Jota turned back to the men and assessed the situation: they were tense, but they wouldn't do anything if he left. It wasn't going to be dangerous. He looked into their expectant eyes, and he realized that he was in danger of ruining the deal. He hesitated. What the hell was that idiot doing there? What did he expect? Then for a moment he thought, *He's on his own; he should know better than to play with fire. A lesson from Rodrigo will do him some good.* But Jota knew that he didn't have a choice. Raul was just a hapless fool and always would be. Cursing Raul and trusting his luck, he spoke to the waiting men.

"Excuse me—this is urgent. I have to go."

Richard turned around in surprise.

"Can't he look after himself? My clients have been waiting for this for a while now."

"Tomorrow: same time, same place. We'll do the deal. I give you my word. Richard, I can't leave him out there on his own. He's like a child—you know that."

He left with Mariano. They headed out onto the street under the irritable gaze of the men, who were waiting to see how Richard was going to react. He shrugged, and they saw they had no reason to wait any longer. They gathered their things and left.

On the street outside the bar, Rodrigo was pressing Raul against a wall, slapping his face, much to the pleasure of an audience that was waiting eagerly for the real violence to begin.

"Didn't I tell you that I never want to see you around here? What have you got, huh? Come on—show me what you're carrying!"

"No, I haven't got anything. I don't do that anymore."

"I've told you a thousand times that you're not welcome here, not you or any of your friends. Did you hear me? There are children here, you know?"

"I don't have anything—"

Jota came running up to separate them. "Rodrigo, leave him alone! He must have come to see me. Raul, did you want to see me?"

"Y-yes, I was looking for you."

The cop was surprised by this new development. "Jota, where did you come from?"

"Rodrigo, let go of him, please. You'll never see him here again—I give you my word. You know they never come around here—"

"They know very well not to come here. I won't be disrespected!"

"Let me deal with this, please. I'll take him away, and you'll never see him again. Come on—go back inside and have a beer. Mariano's already poured it for you."

Rodrigo reluctantly stepped away from Raul, saying, "If I ever see you around here . . . you hear me, Jota? I'm letting him go because it's you, but next time he won't be so lucky, whether you're here to protect him or not."

"There won't be a next time. I promise. Come on—let's go."

Jota walked off, well aware that not only had he endangered the deal but also his relationship with Rodrigo, who turned a blind eye to his activities only because they were old friends. Making a scene like that wasn't a smart move. He was almost as stupid as the idiot he'd pulled to one side, mumbling to himself. They went on a few paces, and he hissed at Raul, absolutely livid.

"I hope you're happy. You've screwed up a deal. And you'd better hope that you've seen the last of Rodrigo."

They walked for several blocks. Raul didn't even dare to touch his face for ten minutes. His cheek was swollen, and when he finally noticed, he was overcome with a feeble fit of rage.

"Who does he think he is? Who does he think he is?"

"A cop. And you're a moron. What were you doing there?"

"I can go where I like. It's a free country."

"Shut up and keep walking. You're going to go wherever he tells you, just like you always have, and you're going to keep your mouth shut."

"He's a dick. The guys at the park have him in their pocket."

Jota smiled at his bravado. That was life in a neighborhood where people like Raul would never leave. They were rotting away in their depressing everyday routine, but still they put on a front. They created a public persona for themselves, trying to seem more interesting or at least more acceptable. Flimflam merchants trying to cheat people who knew them only too well. That was how the neighborhood had descended into hellfire, a slow-drip torment of unsatisfying lives.

"The guys in the park are the dicks. They're full of it until there's actually any danger. Then they run away like cowardly little shits, just like you. And you still haven't said thank you. Or told me what the fuck you want from me."

"I wanted to help you. I heard you were looking for something. I can help."

"You, help me? Tell me—what is it that I'm supposed to be looking for?"

"I heard that you need a clock and—"

"Who told you?"

"No, I just heard. Nobody told me anything."

"Who did you hear it from?"

"In . . . the store, the other day."

"I see."

Raul wasn't going to tell him anything; he would never intentionally reveal his source. Jota thought it might be Torres or his foreman maybe. But they wouldn't care about the clock. Who could possibly be leaking that information? He sized up Raul, wondering what he might be expecting in return. What could possibly be important enough to make him risk Rodrigo's wrath?

"What do you have for me?" Jota said.

"Well, I think I can help you . . ."

"How?"

"Uh . . . I just need to know . . ."

Jota realized that these weren't Raul's words at all. Someone had told him what to say. Someone who wanted to find out about his commission. Now he had to play a tedious game of cat and mouse to lead them back into their own trap. It irritated him to have to be wasting time on such nonsense.

"Well? You've come looking for me, so you must have something to tell me, not questions to ask. Isn't that right?"

"Yes, of course."

"So let's hear it."

"Hear what?"

"What you've got, Raulito! What have you got?"

"No . . . I . . . not here. At home. I have it at home."

"Fine, let's go see it."

"What?"

"I want to see what you have."

"No, but . . ."

"Now!"

"Yes, yes, of course . . ."

Raul's pace slowed the closer they got to his apartment, but they finally arrived at the *corrala*, a nineteenth-century residential building for workers that recently had been saved from ruin by a rebuild that replaced the classic wooden pillars with steel. It was a beehive of claustrophobic apartments set out around a large central courtyard with a shared entrance and, until a few decades ago, a shared bathroom for each floor. A relic from the city's industrial past. They went up a floor, and Raul went into a small apartment where an elderly lady was watching TV.

"Hi, Ma."

"Hello, Son. Listen to what Marimar told me. Do you remember her little boy, the boy they caught stealing?"

Raul walked between her and the TV, ignoring her. "Oh, Ma. Leave me alone. I have things to do."

Jota stood waiting at the door. The mother turned toward him mistrustfully, but when she recognized him, her face lit up with joy. "Oh, it's you! What a surprise! Raul, why didn't you tell me you were bringing guests? I need to get ready. He's going to think we live like gypsies."

She tried anxiously to get up, but with her swollen legs it was a major effort.

"Good afternoon, Doña Asunción. Don't worry about me; I'm not staying long. How are you?"

"Oh dear, that boy of mine is nothing but trouble."

"I'm sorry to hear that. But you're looking younger every time I see you."

"Oh, you old flatterer, you."

Raul came back in to interrupt. "Ma, we're leaving."

"Are you going to your aunt's house? What do you have stashed away in there? You're taking advantage of the fact that I can't climb stairs. Hey, Son! What time should I make dinner?"

"Oh, what do I know, Ma? Leave me alone!"

Jota followed Raul, who had hesitantly headed up the stairs.

"Your aunt is still letting you use her shitty apartment?"

"She died. But my cousins are squabbling over the inheritance, so I'm fine. They haven't been by in years."

They went into a similarly sized but far more run-down apartment. The walls were flaking, and the electricity was out. Raul pulled up the wooden shutters to let in the sun, and the dust rose in golden spirals, giving the place a grimy gleam. The aging wallpaper was rotting with damp while the crumbling ceiling plaster had come right away to reveal old wooden beams. In the middle of the living room was a chaotic pile of dirty, broken things, along with moldy pizza boxes and bottles.

"Fucking hell, it stinks in here. Open a window, you filthy bastard. How can you live like this?"

"I barely ever come here anymore. I just use it to keep old things. I keep the stuff I'm selling now in my bedroom, but here I have . . . I have what you're looking for. Look."

He showed him an alarm clock from the forties that Jota eyed dubiously.

"If you'd brought it by six months ago, we might have bought it. But you know that it's not what I'm looking for. Come on—show me why you brought me here."

Raul started to sweat. He tried to say something, but he stumbled over the words. He bent down to scour through the mess and eventually came up with a shoddy old clock mechanism.

"Look at this. It must be worth something."

But Jota wasn't looking at the clocks—he was looking at Raul. The junkie continued his rummaging, acutely aware of Jota's gaze. He was almost crippled with nerves.

"Raul."

Raul tried to ignore him, but he was in a panic. "Yes, just a moment."

"Raul!"

He turned around, trembling like a little boy caught doing something naughty. "Yeah?"

"You have no idea what I'm looking for, do you?"

"No . . . well, I do. I know that it's a clock."

"But to show me something, you need more information, don't you? You need me to explain what I'm looking for, to give you a photo or a detailed description. To give you an idea of what to look for, right?"

"Yes, exactly."

"Well, Raul. It seems to me that we've been here before."

Raul trembled harder.

Jota kept up his pretense at friendliness. His cool but casual tone only scared his companion more. "Yes, of course. Then you'll ask me to tell you who the client is so you'll know what they might be interested in, how you can help with the commission. Whoever wrote the script for you knew what they were doing. The problem is that you don't. Raul, would you like to know the kind of client that commissioned me?"

"No, no, I wanted to help you . . . maybe I don't have . . ."

"This is your last chance to tell me who the hell told you that I was looking for a clock and who sent you to get information out of me."

"N-no, I . . . heard people talking—"

Suddenly Jota grabbed Raul by the neck and shoved him against the wall. The frail man coughed a couple of times.

"Who the hell told you I was looking for a clock? Who the fuck is trying to get information out of me?"

"No, really—"

"Tell me who sent you!"

"Diego, it was Diego."

"After everything I've done for you, this is how you repay me. You son of a bitch!"

He punched Raul hard in his solar plexus. The junkie doubled over, gasping for breath.

"That piece of shit sent you. The bastard has no idea what kind of trash he's getting to do his dirty work."

"I'm sorry. I didn't think it was a big deal."

Jota shoved him aside with his foot so he could get out. "Now I'm going to visit your boss. You've chosen the wrong side."

"It was just a job. I'm still on your side."

"Don't ever come near me again, or I swear I'll smash your fucking head open. You hear me?"

And without waiting for an answer, Jota slammed the door behind him. The very name *Diego* had him raging inside. Diego the traitor, Diego the bastard, Diego his former friend and partner, the man who owed him for everything he had. The man who he might once have sold his soul for just to get him out of a jam. Diego, the man who had blocked his final chance to escape hell. The flames had risen up to his eyes. He felt the pain in his skin, burning, scarring, scorching right into his soul. Having worked himself up into a rage, he went to see his former partner, whom he hadn't seen in years. Diego never should have stuck his nose into his business again.

He walked purposefully to an antiques store similar to his friend's, only larger and better looked after. In faded lettering, its sign read, **Blanco Collectors, Decorative Art, and Antiques**. Ready for anything, he checked that he had his stubby knife in his pocket and pulled open the door violently. To his surprise, he was met by a young girl at the counter. She looked up from the magazine she was reading, startled. Laura stared back at him in surprise; she had no idea what to say to this brusque apparition. She looked painfully similar to her mother, almost identical to how the woman had been when she was Laura's age: the same disconcerting gaze; the same smooth, aggressive profile; the same beauty. They both stared at each other, feeling as though they were standing before a ghost. He looked at the girl and for a moment was transported back a quarter century. In that fraction of a second, the time it took him to blink, she was almost certain that he recognized her. It was all she needed to recover her composure and youthful insouciance.

"What on earth? Don't you know how to open a door?"

For the first time in many years, as long as he could remember, Jota didn't know what to do with himself. "Uh . . . sorry. I'm looking for Diego."

"He's in the back, but after that racket you made I'm sure he'll be here soon."

A man about Jota's age came down a hallway at the rear of the store. He was thickset and bald with a tired, feeble gait. The antiques dealer was shrouded in a halo of weakness; he'd lost too many battles in his life. Diego bore a haunted look, as though he just wanted it all to be over as soon as possible. But now, a dangerous ghost from his past was standing in front of him. Diego Blanco stood stock still and tensed up, and for a moment no one said a word. He subconsciously took a pen out of his pocket and started playing with it.

"Have you met my daughter?"

"No, Mr. Tough Guy doesn't remember me."

Jota was still unnerved by the girl's attitude. It seemed to drain the moment of its former intensity. Her brazen nonchalance had changed things entirely. It made her both more and less like her mother; she had the same ability to capture people's attention, to mold the situation to her whims. But her mother had been darker. She'd never been so laid back.

"Hello, Laura. Of course I remember you, but you were very young then. I didn't know you'd come back . . ."

"Why are you here?" Diego said, clearly irritated.

And with that Jota felt that he was back on firmer ground: danger and the prospect of violence. He fixed his cold eyes on Diego and let the adrenaline build up once more.

"Tell the girl to leave. I don't want her to hear this."

"She can hear it. Laura, this man has come to fight me. You can leave if you like."

Laura suddenly found the scene incredibly amusing, as such situations often were to the young.

"Really? Ha! I'm staying," she declared, her voice dripping with irony. "But you're both too old for that shit. Even you, hair or no hair."

"I see you've got bored of torturing your mother. Picked a new victim, have you?"

"My mom is on her honeymoon in Bali. But he has trouble admitting it. Are you going to punch him?"

Jota ignored her and spoke to Diego, but the anger had leached out of his voice. Something about the girl's stupid jokes had defeated a hatred that had been nursed for many, many years. He was surprised to find that he had no idea how to deal with it.

"Raul called you, didn't he?"

"You and your partner are looking for a clock. I only did what you would have done. Raul's an idiot. I didn't want to steal anything from you. Just to know if you'd found it."

"Why do you care?"

"That's my business. I'm not getting involved in your affairs ever again. So let's get things straight between us here and now."

Jota could smell Diego's fear. He was lying. He lied about everything but was afraid of physical pain. His cowardice had always held him back. This was Diego, Diego the traitor, the pathetic specimen who was always a step behind everyone else. But Laura's cheek came between the two of them again.

"Are you going to hit him?"

She was the exact opposite of her father. She was like a negative of him. Her mother's wild nature didn't appear to have left room for any of him. And she was much the better for it.

"I see that you take after your mother. I imagine you'd rather be having fun in Bali."

She gave him a playful, amused look. She knew that he remembered her, and something about the way he had seemed so bamboozled when he'd initially seen her was endearing. Very endearing. Without realizing it, she became flirtatious, charming, and just a little dangerous.

"There are other ways to have fun."

Jota ignored her adolescent teasing. He could see no reason to be there anymore. Laura had exposed the absurdity of the situation with her smart-ass sense of humor. She was just like her mother. Somehow,

Laura had put out the flames. He was beginning to feel ridiculous; he needed to get out of there.

"Diego, if I ever hear from you again, I'll come back. And then, I swear I'll kill you, whether she's here or not."

She curtsied like a ballerina. "Why, thank you."

Jota left the store, and Diego sighed with relief. He stopped playing with his pen. Laura gave him the kind of judgmental look that only children could give their parents.

"Did you lie to him?"

"I don't want you ever to mention it again."

"But you used to be friends."

"We were never friends."

Diego stalked out back. Laura tried to go back to her magazine, but she was excited and, to her surprise, very happy. Yes, her heart was beating faster; she was happy to have seen him, but she had no idea why.

Every morning, in Madrid's humbler plazas, from La Latina to Atocha Station, improvised markets manned by old people and petty thieves sprang up, filled with worthless books, recently stolen items, and even tins of food taken from nearby supermarkets. The customers were of the same ilk as the vendors. Jota and Adolfo knew them well and always said hello as they passed by. Today, however, Jota didn't feel like talking and just raised a limp hand. He was worried that his commission had become common knowledge. He'd had a big argument with Adolfo about it. It was when things went wrong that the fissures in relationships started to become apparent. Jota knew that his partner had the trickier hand to play: he had to talk to all his contacts to get information. Could it have been Torres? Why would Torres call Diego? Jota blamed Abdelazil, saying, "He must have been paid off, like Raul." But Adolfo insisted that that was impossible. What was really getting to Jota, although he refused to accept it, was having met Laura's daughter.

She looked the same as Laura had at that age. She even shared the same name. She was just like her.

Driven by some unknown urge, Jota spent the next two days in local bars, "socializing." The work had stalled, not because of any inherent difficulty but because Jota had simply stopped. He spent the time between lunch and dinner drinking gin and tonics. He might have called it socializing, but his friends didn't find him to be particularly sociable. Jota had plenty of inner demons, and when he didn't want to talk, he really didn't want to talk. They'd learned that well. He simply drank his drinks, met up with the odd old flame—or thought about trying to find a fleeting new one in the hope that eventually everything would go back to normal. It was best just to leave him alone. They'd seen it all before, like everything else that happened in the neighborhood. No one ever interfered; things just happened the way they were meant to happen.

One night, Jota woke up with a pain he hadn't felt in years. He felt his side, touching an old scar that had been coarse, dead skin, numb to the touch. But now it was throbbing like it had when it was new.

Five days later, Jota was sitting in the Castillo de Loarre in the middle of the afternoon, on his third drink. It was early; none of his friends had arrived yet, just a couple of men in suits drinking coffee and talking failed deals and deals they hoped would fail. It was bad times all around: everyone was affected, and no one had any problem commiserating.

An hour later, the two men had gone. In their place were three colleagues having a beer after work and two women drinking coffee, criticizing absent friends. Mariano came out from behind the bar with a fresh drink to replace the one Jota had finished.

"Thanks, but I'm going."

"Sure you are."

Mariano discreetly looked up at a young girl through the window. She was heading for the bar. Immediately after closing the door behind her, she looked a little disoriented. Eventually, she asked for the cigarette machine.

"It's over there."

Jota didn't need to look up to know that Laura was there. She was clumsily trying to buy herself a pack of cigarettes. It was an obvious pretext. She stammered a couple of times but finally got out a greeting. Her voice wavered at first, but then she grew more confident.

"Hi, I'm Laura. I was at my dad's store the other day. You know, when you threatened to kill him?"

"Yes."

"Do you mind if I hang out a little?"

"No."

"I've been here for about a month."

Jota played along without saying a word.

"I'd never seen you in the store before."

Jota gave her a brief look and drank his drink.

"But you used to go there all the time when I was little."

"Yeah."

"You're not very much fun."

"No."

"Have you always been this boring?"

Jota looked her in the eyes, and after a longer pause than was necessary, he answered, "Yes."

"That's not true. I remember you. You were always coming and going, and it was like a party whenever you were there."

"I suppose."

"So what happened?"

Jota sighed. His patience was beginning to run out. The girl was irritating, but it was even more irritating to know that really she wasn't bothering him at all.

"Huh. I thought you were going to say something funny."

"Nope."

Laura made as if to leave, but at the last moment she changed her mind and turned to him, clearly annoyed. "You used to have a girlfriend."

"Yes."

"So did she die or just leave you?"

Jota turned to her slowly. His vision was blurry. Laura's eyes welled up too as she realized what she'd just said. The same habit of thinking just after she'd spoken. She drove him crazy just like her mother used to.

"I was wrong the other day. Your mother had a lot of class. You're more like your father: a nasty piece of work."

Laura trudged to the exit in silence. She went out, stopped, changed her mind, and then came back in. Then she went back out again with a snort and tried to slam the door behind her, but the hinges slowed it down. She struggled with it for a little while before finally leaving in humiliation. Jota waited until she was out of sight.

"What do I owe you? I'm going."

"Was that Diego's girl? I thought she lived with her mother."

"So it would seem. Has she come in before?"

"No, but she's hovered around the door a few times. I thought she was planning to steal something, but it seems she wanted to speak to you. Have you been to see Diego?"

"We had words."

"She looks just like her mother, doesn't she? Forget about her, Jota. You shouldn't be getting mixed up in all that."

"I know."

Jota left the Castillo de Loarre, treading wearily. He should've been somewhere else. For the past few days all he had been trying to do was deaden his mind. But Jota had been kidding himself. Her presence took him back in time to the gleam of flames in teenage eyes that had disappeared decades ago. But Jota knew that these eyes were different.

It wasn't the girl but the image, a feeling frozen in the air. It transported him back to that spring. He needed to forget all about it and get back to the commission: it was the only thing that mattered. But reality could be stubborn.

Around the next corner he found Laura sitting in a doorway, smoking. He was surprised to see her, but after their eyes met briefly, he ignored her and continued on his way. Her eyes followed him, pleading. As he passed by, she stood up quickly and followed him.

"I'm sorry! Really, but you were getting on my nerves."

He continued walking.

"You could at least stop."

He did, but only to give her a cold look. She shrank back.

"But you were mean too."

Jota started off again.

"My father had the clock you're looking for!" Laura shouted.

But he didn't stop. He was glad that the girl had her own voice, that she had a distinctive personality. That she was real. In her effort to get his attention, she was revealing the real Laura behind the mask.

"It's true! I have the papers!"

This brought him to a halt. For this version of Laura he was all ears. Now he had to reassess what he thought of her. She'd found her own way to get him to focus and listen. The girl's personality was just as strong as her mother's but very much her own. He liked that. This new young player wasn't just trying to catch his eye; she was telling the truth. It was clear from her voice: she really did have what he needed. For some reason she wanted a role in the game, and that interested him. He looked at this new Laura for the first time. *She has balls*, he thought. *Just like her.* But also she was different.

"What do you want?"

"To talk."

"Did you bring the papers?"

She nodded like a little girl.

"OK, let's talk. Come on. Lead the way."

"Where?"

"Wherever. Somewhere I can have a look at them."

"I know somewhere my father and your friends would never go."

After he refused to take a taxi, they went on a short bus ride that left him completely disoriented. They got out at a main street and went to a place that Jota regarded with the disapproval of a parent confronted with their child's taste in music. It was a modern designer café full of teenagers and the odd family: pastel shades and a wide range of different coffees and diner-style desserts. He immediately regretted letting the girl choose the place. When he sat down and saw the menu full of different colors and images, he felt like throwing it out the window. For the first time, he began to find the situation amusing. She was truly exasperating, just like her mother. While she looked through dozens of pictures of glasses brimming over with cream and cherries, he began to smile for the first time. They both ran their finger down the page in the same way and were quick to anger in just the same way. He was grateful to be able to experience this moment. He'd just discovered the gift of being able to relive an old memory stress-free and realized how lucky he was to have this Laura sitting in front of him. She was new life, with all its ups and downs.

A waiter about the same age as Laura came over, and Laura pointed at a picture no less absurd than any of the rest.

"I'd like a chickcoffee with chocolate topping."

Jota discreetly pushed the menu to one side and coughed, trying to think of something to order. "Errr . . . do you have draught beer?"

"Light or dark?"

"Light."

The waiter went off, and they sat in silence for a moment.

"Do you really have your father's papers?"

"Uh-huh."

"Does your father know?"

"Of course not."

"And how do you know they're related to the clock I'm looking for?"

"I can't say. But you know I have them—otherwise you wouldn't be here."

"You think you know everything."

"Do I take after my mother or father?"

"How do you get on with your mother?"

"Badly."

"Then you're just like her."

Laura's face lit up. She was barely on speaking terms with her mother. But Laura had managed to reach Jota, even if it was only from afar. For a moment she felt like they shared the same space, and she found that both exciting and reassuring.

"Who did you meet first? Mom or Dad?"

"I can't remember."

"I thought you were going to be a little more talkative."

"But it's true. We grew up together. I honestly can't remember."

"Do you mind if I ask why you stopped coming to visit?"

"Do you remember that?"

"A little . . . I was very young. Everything that happened before the divorce is jumbled together."

"It was just business. Don't get the wrong idea—this is all just business."

"This conversation included."

"No, this conversation is free. If your papers are genuine, I'll pay you what they're worth, whether you like it or not. That's how we're going to do it. I won't owe you anything."

"Here, take as much time as you like. I photocopied them in secret."

Laura took a folder out of her backpack and gave it to him. Inside were three photocopies: the first was a delivery note with a photograph of the clock and several handwritten annotations; the second was a spreadsheet with names, prices, and dates, almost all of them crossed out; and the third was a receipt with the note "Santander clock" signed by Diego dated two months after the first. Jota absorbed this information in silence.

"Your father is incredible. He was always writing everything down. But he must have thousands of files. How did you find these?"

"I didn't have to find them. He took them out before you came. You were right—he knew about the deal. It wasn't just about whether you'd found it or not."

"I don't think he knows who bought it. Things like that don't get written down."

"Yeah, he doesn't know. Why does he want to get involved in your business? You're even, aren't you?"

"In my business, you only ever find the thing you're looking for one in a hundred times. Usually you have to make it yourself, and now that I have your father's papers, that's going to be very easy. That's why I thought he might beat me to it, but now, you're right—we're even. I'm the one who knows how to make things, not your father."

"When you say *make*, you mean *forge*, don't you?"

"No, I mean *make*. But why did you do this? You know you've screwed him, don't you?"

"He wasn't very nice to you the other day. He deserves it. Also," she said, smiling slightly, "this way you won't have to kill him."

"Yeah, I know you were worried about that."

She laughed. "See? You can be funny when you want to be." She took a few coins out of her pocket. "I need to be somewhere."

"Obviously I'm not going to let you pay."

"Thank you. Maybe we can see each other again. I like hearing your stories."

"I need to pay you for your work. You did a good job."

"Sure, see you later. Bye!"

Laura dashed out of the café and headed down the street, turning back several times to look at him. When she got to the end, she stopped to keep watch, but he didn't follow her. Then she happily continued on her way.

That night, Jota sat at his worktable drinking beer and studying Diego's paperwork. His former partner was as diligent as ever. Everything was there, even the photograph of the lot, which he'd taken in his store and was much clearer than the one Morgades had given Jota. Jota knew that his work was almost done. He was surprised by the girl's initiative. She'd just gone ahead and done it. Her energy was a double-edged sword. He went into the dark living room, dropped onto the sofa, and turned on the TV. Having flicked through the channels for a few minutes, he turned it off again. He sat for a while like that, beer in hand. It was the fires that lit up your life that ended up swallowing you whole. A double-edged sword.

The next morning, as he shaved, he prepared himself for the final push. He'd had a rare stroke of luck. Toweling himself off, he heard the front door open and the cleaning lady, whom he'd known his whole life, call out.

"Hello? Are you still in? It was only single locked, so I thought . . ."

"Good morning, Maria. I didn't want to leave before I heard all about your daughter's wedding."

"Oh, we had such a wonderful time, but we'll pay for it. My poor girl. The courtship has come to an end."

"The good times are over."

"Now comes the suffering. But we all have to go through it. That boy . . . I just hope they give me a grandchild soon."

Jota got to Velázquez Auction House early, when it was still pretty empty. He said hello to a few employees, not the man who'd seen him the last time, and went straight through to Pilar's dingy back office. Soon she was reading from her screen.

"Yes, it was a small maker in Santander, the kind that copies pieces for second-rate jewelers. Petit bourgeois. I doubt they made anything for anyone outside the city. Maybe someone in Asturias. The industry was much stronger around Bilbao. It disappeared . . . oh, it closed in 1969. I doubt there's anything left. Look." She showed him a couple of images of pieces with the same stamp. "We auctioned off the last two pieces in 2003, and one didn't reach its reserve price. Sent back to the owner. Here." The printer started to spit out pages, making an inordinate amount of noise for its size. "It came from that antiques place in Santander. They still send us things. You could go and use us as a reference."

"No need—I have contacts in Santander. I'll pay you after I've made the delivery."

"Don't worry. These contraptions aren't worth anything. As you've seen."

Jota returned her complicit smile.

The rest of the work was done at Adolfo's shop: reaching out to Santander, checking the maker's mark, finding out what different pieces were available, and arranging accommodation. As usual, his friend took care of the logistics. In the afternoon, once all the arrangements had been made, he came back tired and fairly satisfied. He'd have to get the car fixed up before heading north. A voice surprised him at the front door. Laura was standing on the other side of the street. She ran over.

"Hello!"

Jota's feeling of complacency was shattered. Laura was suddenly there, at the door of his house. She'd broken the rules. Her now-familiar but still irritating lack of respect had seen her blunder into his territory like an overenthusiastic puppy. Jota didn't like it; he felt violated.

"What are you doing here?"

"Well, we never made any plans, so I thought I'd pass by . . . this is where you live, isn't it?"

"How long have you been waiting?"

"A while. Aren't you going to invite me in?"

Jota looked around uncomfortably, feeling exposed. He decided that it was best to continue the conversation in private. "You'd better come up."

They walked up the old staircase in silence. Laura eagerly took in everything. When he opened the door, a huge golden cat turned to stare at them from the end of the hall.

"I didn't know you had a cat," Laura said.

But when the cat's eyes met Jota's, it hissed and ran out through a door. Jota threw a pack of cigarettes after it.

"The little shit! No, I don't have a cat. The bastard breaks in when I'm not here."

Laura's face lit up with a huge smile. "I don't believe you. How long has it been doing that?"

"Six years."

She was stunned. The math didn't add up. Six years? "I don't mean to be nosy, but didn't you . . . ?"

Jota headed into the kitchen without giving her time to finish.

"Would you like anything to drink?"

"Nothing, thank you."

"How did you know where I lived?"

"I came a few times when I was little. But you don't remember, obviously."

"You came here?"

"Yes, with my father. The summer that my grandmother died."

"I remember. You have to have something to drink."

"No, really, I'm fine. Thank you."

"Here, have a beer."

Jota came back with a couple of bottles.

"Mom had to go take care of her, and Dad couldn't leave me alone. You were doing a deal together, so he brought me along."

"Yes, I suppose. I barely remember anything from that summer."

"You had an altarpiece from a church or something."

Jota opened his eyes wide at the forgotten memory. "The diptych. You're right. I'd completely forgotten. The hermit diptych. That was a good story. It never went anywhere near a church; it was falser than Judas. A gay couple from the Netherlands thought they were screwing over a hermit from Bierzo. It's probably in a private museum now. Fuck them."

"I used to love coming here. You always had something for me: chocolate, candy, toys, or whatever."

"That was probably Maria. She loves kids. She kept the drawers full of candy just in case."

"She was lovely, like a fairy godmother. Is she still around?"

"Yes, she still comes. That hasn't changed. You're right—you used to come with your father . . . you'd stay here while we worked in the office. That was our last deal together."

"You were like my . . . my dad looked up to you . . . you have no idea what that means to a girl. You were larger than life. I was so excited to come. Also, while you locked yourselves away, I could look through your old magazines. Some of them had drawings and photos of nudes. I loved them."

"What?"

"Every time I came, I hoped you'd leave me alone so I could look at them. I knew it was naughty, but that made it more exciting. I'd look through them, listening in case the door to your office opened."

"You're kidding. That's ridiculous. You used to come to my house to look at nudie magazines?"

"Don't underestimate the curiosity of children."

"You're shitting me. They must have been *Paris Hollywoods*. You used to read *Paris Hollywoods* while we worked."

"It was all I could think about. I always wanted to go back so I could read more. Then I'd tell my friends at school. I was the coolest kid on the playground."

Jota tried to finish his beer without realizing it was already empty. But that gave him an excuse to get up and look for another. She tried to finish hers to keep up, but it was still half-full. A few moments later, he came back in with an envelope.

"Here, this is yours."

She took it obediently but didn't dare open it. "I can't accept it. I didn't do it for . . ."

"It's not a gift. It's your fee."

"Oh, but . . . no, I don't want it. What will I do with it?"

"Count it."

She looked inside the envelope more out of embarrassment than curiosity. "But this is a lot of money!"

"It's payment for information given. You earned it."

"No, really. Hmmm, I . . ."

"You finished your beer. I'll bring another."

As he went out, she counted the bills and put away the envelope, still stunned. He came back with another bottle.

"Really, I can't accept . . ."

"Forget it—it's done."

They both went quiet for a moment. She decided to steer the conversation back to what interested her. "What deal was it?"

"What deal was what?"

"You mentioned it the other day: the deal that split up you and Dad."

"I stopped caring about that years ago," Jota said with feigned disinterest.

"I didn't."

"Then ask your father."

"He never mentioned you again."

"He thought that I'd stolen from him; I thought he'd screwed me over. Friendships often end under such circumstances."

"Who was right?"

"Neither of us, maybe."

"Did you steal from him?"

"No."

"Did you lie to him?"

"Yes."

"About what?"

Jota gave her a blank look.

"Sorry, it's none of my business . . . you can at least tell me whether Mom knew."

"What?"

"Did she know about the deal?"

"I don't know . . . how should I know?"

To Jota's surprise, Laura's expression darkened as though she were suddenly weighed down by an old but familiar burden. "Do you know the state we were in when they split up? We had nothing. She never went back. I didn't see Dad for three years."

"I don't know anything about that."

"Did you know she was depressed? We lived alone for four years. It was a bad time. We barely had enough money for rent. Things were almost unbearable. We didn't speak for months. Then she found a job, and it got easier. I don't think she slept with anyone that whole time. In the end the people she worked with made her go to the doctor, and the doctor sent her to a psychiatrist. She had to take pills for years. Then she met her boyfriend. Did you know that?"

"No."

"You never saw her again either."

"That was a long time ago. You're too young to be obsessed with the past."

"It was my childhood."

Jota got up and looked at his watch. This seemed a good time to bring the conversation to an end. "It's getting late."

Laura paid no attention. She was lost in her memories. "What was my mom like?"

"Don't you live with her?"

"What was she like when she was young?"

"Young."

"I mean before she got bitter."

Jota didn't want to go back, and certainly not in the company of this kid. He couldn't take responsibility for someone else, someone so young and bereft that she thought he was someone to look up to. Over the last few weeks, his past had been resurfacing, and it was taking more of a toll than he cared to admit.

"Finish your beer. You should be getting back."

"I want another."

"You've had enough."

Jota got up and left again, but he didn't come back into the living room. He stood by the door. "Come on. You'd better get going before your father starts to worry."

"Why won't you answer me?"

"Why are you asking me? Ask your parents."

"Because you'll tell me the truth."

"I don't know the truth."

"Yes, you do. You owe it to me."

He slammed his beer bottle down on a shelf, making a sharp sound. Foam overflowed from the mouth, covering his hand, but he didn't seem to notice. His voice remained cold. "I don't owe you anything. I thought we made that clear right from the start."

"I-I'm going," she stammered, getting up and gathering her things.

She passed him by without looking at him. He didn't move. He heard her opening and closing the door out onto the street. He still didn't move.

The afternoon grew slow and sticky. He finished the bottle of gin and walked aimlessly around the house like a caged animal. The flames were rising around him, close enough that he could hear them crackling, consuming the beauty of his youth. Eventually, he picked up a jacket and went out. Ignoring the buzzing in his head, he headed for the Castillo de Loarre. It would be a fateful trip.

He entered and said hello to the cardplayers. Rodrigo wasn't among them. He sat at the bar, where two men gave him a nod of recognition. He looked toward the other end of the bar, where Gabriel, Rafa's assistant, was sitting on his own, reading the paper. Gabriel, the guy who'd beaten up Raulito. Miriam's lover, the rat who'd come up in life clinging to the back of Rafa, another opportunist. The great Rafa, the customs agent who worked with China and ran almost the entire import market on his own. The man who monopolized his suppliers and only rarely agreed to share them. Neither of them was welcome in the world of old-time dealers, or the few that were left, at least.

"Good evening, Jota," Mariano said, coming over to serve him. "The usual?"

"Strong and no ice. I have a sore throat. What's he doing here?"

"He knows he shouldn't be here. Ignore him; he's not bothering anyone. Rafa did a deal with the guys you were meeting with the other day. He's come to collect a payment, but they haven't turned up yet. I don't want any trouble, OK?"

"Was that my deal?"

"You knew what would happen if you walked out. Richard tried to back you up, but they wanted someone else."

"Of course, you and Richard were powerless to act . . . where's Rodrigo the supercop?"

"He's working. He won't be coming in tonight."

“Of course.”

It was so easy to screw up a deal. All it took was a fucking junkie turning up at exactly the wrong time. But how could Richard have let this guy get involved? Before he knew it, he was standing by the card-players’ table with a gin and tonic in his hand. He began talking loudly.

“This is a bar for men, not motherfucking pansies. If your boss doesn’t have the balls to come in here, he shouldn’t be sending you. That’s a coward’s move.”

The players laughed mockingly along with him. Gabriel didn’t even look up. In his mind’s eye, Jota saw Adolfo shut away in his shop and Gabriel coming out of a seedy hotel that Miriam had probably paid for. He kept staring until the kid couldn’t ignore him anymore and returned the gaze. This was what Jota had been waiting for.

“What?”

“What the hell is wrong with you?”

The cardplayers were enjoying the standoff, and they didn’t hesitate to stir the pot.

“Oooh, be careful—he’s getting his panties in a twist.”

The whole table laughed maliciously, staring at Gabriel. Mariano came out from behind the bar, annoyed.

“That’s enough. Gabriel, go. I’ll keep the money for you. Come back tomorrow morning. I told your boss that you can’t do business here.”

“What the fuck? No one throws me out. I don’t care where I am.”

The cardplayers took their cue.

“Run along home, little boy.”

“I’m not bothering anyone. This isn’t your fucking bar.”

“And it’s not your whorehouse,” Jota said, “the one you’re running with Rafa.”

They confronted one another, their fixed gazes cold and tense.

“Oh, that’s right. You’re not the only one fucking Diego’s whore of a daughter.”

Before anyone could react, Jota had taken out his knife, and Gabriel had jumped up, ready for a fight. Mariano stood in Jota's way.

"What the hell is wrong with you? I don't want any trouble."

Gabriel went on goading him, and Jota stepped closer, enjoying the rage bubbling up from inside of him. *That's right—you tell people that it's about the girl. Tell them it's about Diego's daughter.* He was enjoying feeling the worst parts of himself come to the fore, savoring the violence, the prospect of doing harm and getting hurt in turn.

"I'm not afraid of you," Gabriel said, standing his ground. "I'm right here."

"Shut up, damn it!" Mariano said. "Jota, give me that."

Jota let his friend take the weapon and suddenly seemed to calm down.

"Come on—let me get you another drink. Gabriel: get out. I won't say it again."

Gabriel headed for the door, enraged.

In the blink of an eye, so fast that it took everyone by surprise, Jota grabbed the bottle from Mariano's hand and took a couple of steps toward Gabriel, who only barely had time to raise his arms to protect himself. The first blow hit him on the forearm, and the second hit him right on the forehead, drawing blood. Jota smiled and relished the malice rising up the back of his neck. *Let them think this is about the girl.* His excitement was burning red hot. *Let them think that.* Gabriel stumbled backward, and Jota hit him again and again on the head. Now his entire scalp was bloody. Deep down, although Jota didn't want to admit it, it was about her. As the heavy glass club rose and fell, coming down with a crack onto Gabriel's skull, it was about her.

"Fucking hell, separate them!" Mariano shouted.

Jota wouldn't ease up. Mariano grabbed him from behind, but no one else moved. Gabriel tried to stay upright, leaning on a table, his face covered in blood. Mariano pulled Jota away, but he wriggled from his grasp, knocked Gabriel to the ground, and began to kick him. Finally, the cardplayers intervened and pulled him away.

The entire top half of Gabriel's body was soaked in blood.

"Stop—you're going to kill him!"

Three men pinned Jota back. He relented, not wanting to bring them into the fight. He knew that he'd gone too far, that he might have caused serious damage. *Let them think this is about her.* The flames had risen, and they were threatening to swallow him whole.

"Help me get him out of here," Mariano said. "Antonio, close the bar. Fuck, pull down the blinds. We can't let people see this."

Mariano and two others pushed the semiconscious Gabriel out through the back door, crossed the courtyard, and went out into a back alley. After checking that no one was around, they dragged him to an intersection.

"I'm going back," Mariano said. "Leave him on the stairs to the metro. Someone will get him to the hospital."

Mariano got back to his bar, demanding to know where Jota was.

"He went home."

"Oh, for fuck's sake. You didn't even try to stop him. And now you'll all go home happy with the show. Just because Rodrigo wasn't here. Do you think he'd have dared to do that if he were?"

"Well, forget it. There's nothing you can do now."

"You're all bastards. Come on—help me clean all this up. I knew it. I knew it . . ."

The Castillo de Loarre was closed unexpectedly while a frightened old woman informed the guards in the metro that a man covered in blood was languishing on the stairs. After discovering that he wasn't a bum but gravely injured, they called the police.

The only sign of injury to Jota was a bandage on his left hand. He forgot about the fracas immediately; what was done was done. Gabriel never should have been there, and he was nothing to Jota. Miriam and Adolfo were the ones who mattered. He was satisfied with his evening's work. He put the incident out of his mind and started to pack the few things he'd need in Santander, a trip that he didn't expect to last longer than a couple of days.

As he was driving along the smooth landscape of the Castilian plateau, his phone rang. He answered immediately. It was Rodrigo, sounding agitated.

"Jota? Where the hell are you? What the hell happened yesterday? I've got a complaint against you for assault. You broke the guy's nose and cheekbone!"

"Thanks for letting me know, Rodrigo. If Gabriel reported me, he's more of a shit than I thought. I'm on my way to Santander right now. I have some business there."

"Fucking hell, I'm sick of this! What the hell is wrong with you? Have you gone crazy? You need to get back here!"

"Talk to him. The guy's a pansy; he'll withdraw the complaint."

"I can't hear you very well—are you driving?"

Jota laughed mischievously and hung up without answering. The glistening green landscape of the Cantabrian valley reminded him of Ireland. It was easy to see why there was a sense of camaraderie between the two peoples: the shady glens, the shared tradition of fog and mist.

Now, having arrived, Jota was walking with another man in a small town outside of Santander, past rows of small rose gardens with a view of the city across the bay. They went into an old stone house where an elderly man who could barely get up was waiting for them. The man gave him a friendly wave.

"How are you, Don Ramiro? This is the friend from Madrid I was telling you about. The one who wanted to see the pieces from your jewelry store."

"It wasn't mine. It belonged to my grandfather. My dad ran it into the ground, the bastard. He spent it all on whores and cards. My mother had to raise us on her own, and the world wasn't like it is today, when everything's so easy. It was different back then."

The old man displayed the two pieces still in his possession: one was a crystal salad bowl with a silver stand and the other a squat jar. Jota studied them closely. They both had the maker's mark, and both were in a similar style to the photograph of the clock.

"They're very nice. I hear that you're not interested in selling, but I'm sure that we can come to some kind of arrangement."

"My grandfather was a great man. He founded the workshop and earned a lot of money for his children. He did it all for them. But my father ruined it, and he was still around to witness everything go to hell. Now I know how my grandfather felt as an old man. This is all that I have left from the workshop. Do you think I care about money? What good will selling them do me?"

"But you said that we could have the molds," Jota's friend said.

"We won't alter them in any way. They'll be spotless," added Jota.

"Do what you like with them. I don't care."

The two men got to work. While his companion photographed the objects, Jota took two packets out of a suitcase. They looked like white clay. He brushed a liquid onto the stamps of each piece, covered his hands in light powder, and pressed the pieces against the packets, leaving an impression. In all, the process took less than twenty minutes.

Jota and his friend met with another man in the back room of a jewelry store. They were examining some pieces in fairly poor condition. Jota's phone kept ringing throughout their meeting. Finally Jota excused himself to answer it. The men came to a tentative price for two pieces, not that they'd be much use anymore.

"Is this all you have?"

"It's not just what I have—it's what there is. You won't find anything more in Santander or anywhere else."

"I'll take that bet."

Jota came back in with a shocked expression. He gave them the news without revealing any more details, not that he knew them. Diego Blanco, who had been his partner for many years, had been found murdered the night before. He had tried to stop a robbery: there were signs of violence and struggle; the store was smashed up. *How could there have been a struggle?* Diego had always been a coward. But now he had been stabbed to death, and his daughter had found the body.

4

After the wake, which Jota didn't attend, the hearse led the funeral procession onto the highway, as though it were trying to lose them as part of a cruel joke. They headed for the cemetery, where the body was cremated after a mass that Diego never would have wanted. Like many others who had broken off relations with the deceased, Jota still felt obliged to pay his respects. He arrived with Adolfo and sat uncomfortably at the back, by the door. He quickly located Laura without her seeing him. She was unconsciously fiddling with the pen her father used to play with; it was the same tic. She was being consoled by Carlos, Diego's older brother, who looked very much like him; he had a similar face but lighter eyes and plenty of hair. Laura's mother had canceled her trip as soon as she heard the news, but even so she had to fly halfway around the world to get back. Jota wondered if he would have shown if she were there. When was the last time he'd seen her? He tried to remember what she'd said, but the last time they'd seen each other, there had been no words, only cold silence, mute accusation, and guilt. A guilt from which he'd never recover. No, he wouldn't have gone if Laura had been there. For a second Jota thought he could smell her perfume again. A moment's intimacy on a hot summer afternoon, lying in the damp, warm grass, his hand playing with her hair. The memory vanished as quickly as it had arrived. Jota slipped through the crowd to get outside. He stood leaning on a wall, smoking a cigarette.

Laura didn't feel as though she was really there. She wasn't feeling the strong emotions she would have expected, but neither did she feel in control. It was as though she had the flu or was a little drunk. She knew where she was, but everything happening around her seemed like it was being filtered through a plastic screen or a long tunnel. For a moment she thought, *This is OK; it's not so bad*, but suddenly she felt an immense pain in her chest, a devastating anguish that seemed to come from out of the blue. It wasn't associated with a specific thought. This wasn't a direct response to her father's death. She banished the phrase from her mind. For some reason it sounded obscene, like a dirty joke at his expense. She didn't want to hear or even think it: *My father's* . . . and then she was lost in a pit of vague, unconnected thoughts. She had to focus to remind herself that she was really there, right at that moment, at a table her uncle had led her to after the cremation, surrounded by people expressing their sorrow and compassion. But she was still absent, and she knew people could tell from the way they were looking at her. Then she felt an overwhelming urge to leave and went to hide in the bathroom, where she was struck by a new wave of pain. Laura started to sob in silence. She felt like screaming until her lungs burst, but she couldn't, not with everyone there. She had to muffle her sobs.

Jota didn't go to the table, but Adolfo did. He went over to hug Carlos, a friend from his youth, when everything had seemed so much easier.

"Hello, Carlos. How's the girl?"

"I don't know. I'm worried about her. She wasn't very close to her father, but a shock like this . . ."

"Yes. We won't know for a while. I'm sorry. I wanted to give you my condolences. I was at the cremation."

"Thank you. I saw you, but you left before I had a chance to say hello."

"It's incredible, isn't it? We've all been talking about it. In our business, you know: you worry about it, but you still don't expect something like this to happen. What were they trying to steal? People are talking about organizing a protest march against crime and the way the neighborhood is being neglected. But we never thought something like this would happen to your brother."

"Yeah, but the thing is . . . I did expect something like this to happen. He was always caught up in shady business. If it had been the Russian Mafia or something . . . but a shitty pair of petty thieves . . ."

"I don't know if this is the right time to be talking to you about this, but I think he'd changed. He stopped working in those circles years ago. In fact, we've all changed. The neighborhood isn't how you remember it. That's what we've been saying: it shouldn't have happened now, not to your brother. It's wrong, but then we all think we're an exception to the rule . . ."

"Yeah, you always think it's going to happen to someone else."

"Have the police said anything?"

"They say that they can't say anything. It looks like the work of a gang they've been investigating for some time."

"So nothing, then."

"Yeah, nothing."

"But the neighborhood needs to do something. How about you—what are you going to do with the girl?"

"I came to close up the store, and then I'll go home. She'll stay with me until her mother gets here. I'll stay as long as it takes to sell off Diego's things. I'm telling everyone come by to do your deals. I just want to get this over with and leave. I've had enough of this area. We grew up in a fucking shithole. We have to count ourselves lucky that she wasn't there when it happened."

Laura came back out from the bathroom to join them. Her red eyes and the streaks down her face made it clear that she'd been crying. Her uncle tried to hug her, but she gently pushed him away. She just wanted to breathe a little, she murmured, and slipped away into the shadows, trying to work out how to escape her muffled state so she could connect with people again.

Night had fallen when Jota arrived at Castillo de Loarre. He did not bother to greet Mariano, only demanded to be let into the meeting room. There, he asked about what had happened to Diego, what was known, who might have heard something, not because he was really interested but because it seemed the right thing to do. After a desultory conversation, he handed over a bag. Mariano took it in surprise. He looked inside and then back up at Jota.

"Very nice . . . I suppose this is an apology?"

Jota didn't say a word. He just took out a cigarette.

"You abused my trust. This is my home. I don't let anyone settle scores in here, not even you. The next time it happens, you'll be going to the hospital, too, and you won't be allowed to set foot in this place ever again. I mean it."

"You know it won't happen again."

"Do you know what you did to Gabriel? He has to wear a plastic mask."

"Now you can call him the Elephant Man. Did he really report me?"

"Of course not."

Laura was in her father's apartment above the store; she'd been living there for the past few weeks. Every now and again, she remembered what she was doing and went back to packing her clothes. Then she'd forget and start wandering around again. She ended up in her father's room, sat down on the bed, and picked up a brown envelope from the nightstand. It contained what he'd had on him at the time of his death. She opened it and took out a wristwatch, a chain with Christ on the cross, and a leather wallet. The wallet had a photo of her in it. Then she pulled out a page of notes. She spun around when her uncle came in.

"Laura! I'm sorry if I startled you. Your mother must be about to arrive."

Laura stared back at him blankly with the envelope in her hand.

"They gave it to me yesterday." He took the note from her. "It's a receipt for something he never got around to delivering."

She put everything into the envelope as she got up. He handed the note back to her.

"There's always so much one leaves unfinished, honey . . . shall we go?"

"No," she said, her voice trembling. "Can I stay a little longer? On my own, I mean."

"If you like."

Carlos left, leaving Laura staring at her father's things. Her eyes lingered on the note. A sum of €6,000 and a breakdown of the payment: 1,500 on delivery, the rest once it had been authenticated. Over the next hour, Laura unwittingly kept coming back to the page, getting lost in her thoughts, shaking herself out of it, and then drifting away again. Eventually a space in her head started to fill as the minutes went by. Her mind had begun to work at a different speed. A little later she envisioned what was about to happen: her uncle and mother would come up to find that she refused to leave. They might repeat themselves a few times. They'd be worried at first, and then her mother, tired from her journey, would try to take control, assuming that her daughter wasn't thinking properly. She'd have no idea that, in fact, Laura was completely remade. Laura felt whole again. She'd found something important to cling to, a reason for her pain, and a path to sealing the wound—all inside a receipt for two payments. Anyone in their right mind would find it absurd. If she told them what she was planning to do, they'd send her to a psychiatrist, but in spite of her mental breakdown, she was seeing things clearly. Maybe this was the kind of illumination that only came during periods of great stress. Laura was out of herself, and when the pain following the stage of denial arrived, she'd found a perfect excuse to avoid it. She would refuse to accept that her father was gone.

After being trapped in a cloud for two days, her mind was sharp and working faster than normal. She was experiencing the euphoria of a bipolar disorder, the high that came before a deep, dark depression. The euphoria was her trump card, something she'd never even have conceived of a few days earlier. Before they came to pick her up, she called her mother's husband, who was more a father to her than her real one had been, to explain, telling him that there was a boy she cared about who was helping her. She made up whatever she could think of to convince them that it was a good idea for her to stay a few more days or weeks. She began to feel excited again. Although she didn't know it, she was experiencing a state of paranoia that kept her senses alert and instincts keen. She was bathed in the false reassurance of having a mystery to solve, an enigma that would heal the loss that tormented her.

"Hello, you crazy old fool. Look what I have for you," said Jota, entering the old man's clock workshop, carrying a bulky package.

The old man patiently unwrapped a mold for the clock from the photograph made from plaster.

"Here you go: a mold. Now you have your model."

"Oh . . . yes . . . well, I have a lot of work at the moment. Can I keep it for the afternoon to take measurements?"

"This is for you, you silly crank. I need your cousin to make the case; you can find the mechanism. How much will he charge?"

"I don't know. I'll have to ask him. It'll be about . . . three hundred, I suppose . . . if you're in no hurry."

Jota was inspecting three clocks on a shelf. He picked one up and studied it. "Good work, old man."

"Oh, those . . . they're for another job. Commissions for Rafa. You know . . ."

"For Rafa?"

"Yes . . . he brought them from Germany. They're good pieces. I have to get them working perfectly."

"That's what a customs agent is for."

"Well, he moves around a lot these days. He gives me a lot of work. It adds up. Diego's brother is selling everything in the store. Carlitos . . ."

"I heard."

"He's closing it, selling everything, a big sale. Aren't you going? Rafa has bought a lot of lots."

"Adolfo went. I have no business there. That's all over. Over."

When Jota got back to his building, Miriam was waiting for him, staring at him with a hollow look in her eyes. There was no hatred or disgust there, no feeling at all. Her eyes were just dull. Jota realized that anything that had once been between them was dead. He no longer had any kind of relationship with this woman, whom he'd always loved. He was standing in front of Miriam, but she saw nothing. There was nothing for her here.

"It's over, Jota."

"Hello, Miriam. Did you hear about Diego?"

"All I ask is that you don't insult my intelligence. Gabriel was nothing to me, but he didn't deserve that."

"I don't know what bullshit Gabriel's been telling you, but—"

"I haven't seen him. I don't need him to tell me anything. Your fingerprints are all over this. You always need to make your mark. It's a shame, Jota, a shame that you think you're better than us."

"Wait a moment, Miriam. There was something else. It had nothing to do with you."

"I won't stop talking to you, Jota. I'll always say hello. I'm sorry. I'm sorry I ever looked up to a man like you. But most of all I feel sorry for you. You're a pitiful man, and you don't even know it. Now you'll have to choose someone new to protect."

Miriam turned around and disappeared without giving him a chance to answer or explain himself. But Jota didn't try to stop her. He knew that look. He knew that she wasn't just turning her back on him then and there. A past he'd thought long buried had been rearing its head recently, and Miriam was cutting his closest ties to it, closing a door that wouldn't be opened again.

Laura's uncle was getting rid of his brother's things as fast as he could, selling group lots to local antiques dealers who'd come running at the whiff of a bargain. Laura, who seemed strangely full of life, helped him with the administrative chores, doing paperwork that he didn't even realize needed doing. Much more than seemed necessary. On the second afternoon, her uncle questioned her worriedly.

"Are you going to be here all day?"

"I just wanted to help you so I know for sure that he hasn't left any loose ends."

"You can't stay here locked up in the dark. It's not healthy."

"Do you know where my father's last phone bill is?"

"Well . . . we canceled it the day before yesterday. I should have it around here somewhere . . . maybe with the last mail delivery . . . just a second."

He left the room, and she went through her father's planner. He'd written down an appointment under *clock*. The last few pages contained the names and telephone numbers of his contacts. She was hoping to compare them to his most recent phone calls.

Her uncle found the bill, and Laura spent the night preparing a list of people her father had called in the days prior to his death, anyone who might have had a connection to that damned clock. The next morning, she visited the first. The address was far away, in another district: an interior design store with a crudely ostentatious, nouveau riche aesthetic. There, several salespeople in suits and ties, very polite but aloof, escorted her to an upper floor, where she was shown into an office decorated with paintings in golden frames. The man waiting didn't get up to greet her.

"So you're Diego's daughter. Very good. I was sorry to hear about your father. What can I do for you?"

"Well, you and my father spoke a lot over the phone. I imagine you did a lot of business."

"I do a lot of business with your father and a lot of other people. A man in my position deals with everybody. You know what I mean?"

"Yes, but you were doing some business with my father."

"So? What do you want?"

"It's about something he might have offered you."

"You'd better speak more clearly. Your father was a straight speaker; that's why I bought from him."

"But my father never bought anything from you? I think he wanted to get back something that he'd sold."

"Do I look like someone who'd sell back something I'd bought? Do you think I'd need to do that? Listen, girl: this is an ecosystem. You know how ecosystems work? Do you? Like a pyramid—some are at the top and others at the bottom. You know what I'm talking about, don't you? Do they still teach that in schools? I buy things from people below me and so on down to the people who buy things from the elderly and the dead. Your father was toward the bottom of the pyramid. Let me give you a piece of advice: if you want to get something of his back, don't go around telling people that you're looking for it."

That was all Laura needed; she crossed the first name off the list.

Jota went to an estate agency that specialized in small apartments, one of the few that had survived the economic crisis. It had done so by firing the entire staff, leaving just the two owners. Both men were middle aged and wore suits and ties. They spent their days bored and isolated in a tiny office that looked as though it was locked in a state of mourning for better times. They both got up to greet him.

"What a pleasant surprise. No one remembers us paupers anymore."

"How are you doing?"

"What can I say? Surviving."

"And thank goodness for that—we're the only ones around still open."

"For now, at least."

"But we get by; it's one good thing about spending so long in the same place. You get to know everyone."

"Do you have anything for me?"

"We've got a new apartment in: an old woman, no children. The nieces and nephews don't want anything to do with it. They took a table and left the rest for us to deal with."

"Anything good?"

"Old woman stuff. What do I know? That's your department."

"Let's go."

One of them accompanied Jota to the place while the other waited in the office, knowing no one would show up. Old apartments sometimes contained treasures hidden among the dusty furniture and knickknacks. Estate agents were an important part of an antiques scout's network, along with porters and even warehouse guards who diligently reported the entry and exit of goods and were very useful in facilitating the removal of items that wouldn't be missed for months. Jota didn't have many contacts like this left. Today, he didn't find anything. His double take wasn't due to anything inside but the sight of Laura standing at a bus stop. He'd been told that she'd left along with her mother. Barely aware of what he was doing, he surprised the estate agent by heading out to greet her, afraid of missing out on what would probably be his only chance. He knew that he was very unlikely to see her again and moved with an urgency he didn't quite understand. He wondered what he'd say. Offer her his condolences? Just say hello? He was driven by the idea of seeing someone he'd never see again, who tied him to a past that had begun to die with Diego a few days before and which Miriam had so harshly brought to a definitive end. The dark sensation of stepping back twenty-five years, when her mother had been around. But the bus beat him to the stop.

Laura spent several days interviewing people she didn't want to meet and got nowhere. At best they spoke to her as though they thought she was a girl driven mad by her father's death who was now playing detective. At worst, she got propositioned: one man offered her information in exchange for sex and tried to corner her when she said no. She had had to scream to get him to let her out of the office. But at no point did she consider giving up. Eventually, she came to a small shop buried below street level, far away from anywhere. She was met by a frail man who looked older than he was. He was almost certainly past retirement age, but he had incredible energy. The man didn't wait for her to introduce herself; he met her eye and greeted her immediately.

"Good morning. You must be Diego's daughter. I've been expecting you for a few days now."

"Huh . . . do we know each other?"

"I paid my respects at the cremation, but don't worry—I wouldn't expect you to remember. I was very close to your father. He was a gentleman, always. That's why I wanted to introduce myself. I owed him that. Have you come looking for help?"

"Well, yes . . . how did you know?"

"When you get to my age, you know everything. I know that you've been asking about a clock that your father sold, maybe looking for the person who bought it, someone he spoke to recently."

The man shepherded her in, and she had no choice but to obey, wide eyed and confused. "How do you know all this?"

"You're still very young. You have a lot to learn. I wish you'd been more careful. You've been visiting people and asking questions very openly. A lot of people know what you're looking for already. The wrong individuals might get wind of it."

"Then you know what I'm talking about? You know that my father was murdered, that he had enemies? I think he was looking for the clock, and whoever has it didn't want him to find it."

"I know he was murdered. And you want to believe that it was because he was looking for a clock. Listen, I have no idea whether he was looking for a clock because your father didn't share anything with anyone. In fact, I think that he was looking for a lot of different clocks, just like every other antiques dealer. But more than anything I know that you're too young to be going to so much trouble over this."

"So you don't want to help me."

"My father was killed in the war when I was just a child. I had to support my siblings. I started work at a very young age. While I worked, I fantasized that one day I would find the man who'd killed my father and kill him myself. When I grew up, I went back to the village and found that my father had been shot along with a lot of other young men. There wasn't just one guy to kill; it was a bunch of anonymous soldiers. Deep down, I'd known it right from the start, but when someone kills your father, young lady, you want it to mean something, to have someone to blame so that it sits well at the very least. It's horrible to think that thieves killed a good man for a few lousy bucks. It's very good of you to think like that, but you're too young—you can't waste your youth on revenge fantasies, looking for someone who doesn't exist."

"But you just said—"

"That your father ran with a bad crowd who you have no business getting to know, especially if you're acting on your own. I'm not the only one who knows what you're doing. They might already be planning to do you harm, just as they wanted to harm your father. But that doesn't necessarily mean that you're right. Just that if you continue on this path, you'll suffer even more than you're suffering now."

Laura was confused. She didn't think that she understood, or rather she didn't want to. She thought about sleepwalkers and how you weren't supposed to wake them up. Suddenly she felt the entire weight of the loss on her shoulders and realized the old man was right. It was absurd that she'd been trying to uncover an imaginary conspiracy. She tried to thank him and say goodbye, but her voice was trembling, and before she'd even turned around, she broke down into a fit of sobbing, letting out all the pain that had built up in the past few days. The man didn't try to console her. He didn't know how. Laura left the store under the dark gaze of the old man, who was embarrassed by this display of emotion. She couldn't stop crying, but she still tried to walk down the street, breaking up inside, overflowing with tears that burned her like acid. Passersby stared at her, wondering what might have happened.

Several hours later, after getting through the bitterest moments on her own, she went to the boy she'd been with in the park, the one she'd used as an excuse to stay. He was a poor boy to whom she was an enigma. He couldn't help but fall in love with such a mysterious creature, someone who was never really there. She went to him for temporary warmth.

"We could go to my house. My parents won't be back till late."

"I'm sorry. I'm sorry for coming to you like this; please forgive me. I didn't have anyone else to go to."

"You have me—that's all you need. I'll take care of you, protect you."

"No, listen: this is over. Tonight I'm going home to my mother. There's nothing for me here. We can talk later."

"I don't care. I'll go there. I love you."

"You just don't understand."

Laura didn't notice she was being watched. Raul had been waiting for days for someone who could help him without having to leave his home turf. He was wanted by the same people who'd killed Diego. He'd been wandering around, hoping in vain to meet Jota, but Jota was oblivious, preoccupied with the clock, the best deal he'd had in years. Jota wasn't answering his phone or the messages Raul sent; Raul was dead to him. Raul was afraid. When he saw Laura, he thought that she might be able to help. He waited patiently for her to get rid of the boy and approached her when she'd gotten to what he considered to be a discreet location.

Laura was startled to see him, but she recognized him immediately. She knew more or less what he did for her father, but she'd never considered him someone who might know something. His intrusion was as unwelcome as it was unexpected.

"Hello, miss. I'm sorry about your father. He was a friend."

"I know. I know who you are—I saw you with him. I know you started all this."

This unsettled Raul. He didn't know how to begin. Her accusation intimidated him. He laughed nervously but then blurted something that wasn't funny at all. "I know why your father was killed."

Before she could stop herself, a couple of tears were flowing down her cheek, but she got control of herself and stared at him stony faced.

"So do I. It doesn't matter. I don't want any more to do with it. Leave me alone."

"No, please, just give me a minute. I won't tell you anything, and I won't ask for anything. I know that you're a friend of Jota's, and I need to see him. He's the only one who can help me, and since what happened, he's refused to respond to my messages. I can't go there, where the antiques stores are. They're waiting for me."

"I'm sorry. I haven't seen Jota recently, and I'm leaving tonight. Go away."

"He'll listen to you—you know he will. Tell him that I have to see him right away. I'll be waiting for him at eleven at Icaro, a bar a long way from here that only we know. I sent him messages and waited there a few days in a row. He's very angry with me, but he'll listen to you."

"I'm not going to see him. I want you to leave me alone."

But Laura's tone belied her words. Now there was a hint of curiosity in it as she debated between her eagerness to find out more and her need to get away from it all. Something cold inside her told her that either way led to more pain.

"You have to help me. You have to tell him not to look for me at my mother's house. Since what happened to Diego, I've been hiding out. Tell him to go to the Icaro, the same place as usual. He'll know it."

"What's the address?"

"He knows it."

"But I don't. Write it down for me."

"So you'll tell him?"

"Maybe, if I see him."

Raul walked away reassured. He childishly believed that Jota would come to see him that night and that he'd fix everything for him, trusting to the selfishness of people who had long forgotten how to fend for themselves. He couldn't see the difference between a scuffle in the street and a potentially fatal encounter. He couldn't see that the people who killed Diego were smart enough to keep track of him even if he was hiding out in an abandoned apartment. They were just waiting for him to lead them to a bigger fish. They watched him from a car a little way away and were surprised to see him talking to Diego's daughter. They'd ignored her before, in spite of her very public tantrums. Now they anticipated a good catch later that day.

Laura's changing mood swung again. She decided not to talk to her uncle about going home. She even called her mother to explain how right she'd been to stay. Her mother was convinced by the excitement in her voice: it was sincere. The time finally came for their appointment at Icaro. It was closer than Raul had led her to believe, in a dirty, depressing industrial area. At this time of night, it was pretty dangerous. The only people there were a couple of men watching TV in silence and Raul, who was sitting at a table. When he saw Laura arrive instead of Jota, he suddenly realized what anyone else would have seen long ago. Before she could come in, he got up and left, grabbing his head in desperation, mumbling in a hoarse sob: "No, no, no, no, no, no, no, no, no."

Laura followed him and tried to get him to stop, but he wouldn't wait for her.

"Stop for a moment, please!"

"No, no, no, no, no. Why did you do this? He's the only one who can help me. Now what am I going to do? What can I do?"

He continued to ignore her, and when she tried to grab his arm, he shook it away roughly. Raul turned a corner with Laura following close behind, but as she came around, she saw a burly blond man kick Raul to the ground. Before she could react, she was hit in the face. It was little harder than a slap but enough to knock her down. She felt herself being picked up, and another, harder slap left her thinking perfectly clearly and rationally. In that strange state of lucidity, she allowed herself to be taken, aware of her vulnerability while they covered her mouth, dragged her along in silence, and pushed her into the back seat of a car. She could hear the man who'd knocked Raul down beat him some more. Someone, maybe the man who had knocked her down, appeared to accompany the beating with a low whistle, like they were working in a garage. While her hands were tied with plastic strips, Laura heard movement. The other two men were trying to shove Raul into the trunk, talking to each other all the while.

"We were waiting for this piece of shit? I thought someone else was coming."

"So did I. Maybe the little whore knows something."

They got rougher, and Laura heard the sound of a door being slammed repeatedly against a body. Raul made no sound.

"Fuck, this is a motherfucking mess. Fuck this guy . . ."

"Put him in the back. This trunk is a piece of shit. American ones are much better. They know how to make cars."

"This is a Ford."

"Shut up."

Laura's captor was trying to speak over them, whispering to her in a friendly voice: she shouldn't worry; nothing was going to happen to her; they didn't have anything against her. They'd let her go soon. She just had to help them answer a few questions, and then she'd be set free. But then he was interrupted by the others dragging a blood-soaked Raul into the back seat. He gestured to them to cover Raul's bloodied face and put her in the front passenger seat. She felt herself being moved, pushed into a seat, and a seat belt pulled around her. Feeling trapped, she instinctively released the seat belt as soon as the door was closed. Behind her, she heard a moan. She didn't want to think about what they'd done to Raul and didn't dare ask. Laura didn't make a sound or open her eyes until she heard the driver sit down and start the car. Then she saw one of the attackers in the rearview mirror. He'd stayed behind and was headed back into the bar, perhaps just in case someone else showed up. In the back she could see a head but not Raul. Then she heard a muffled moan and realized that he must be on the floor. The blond man, who was driving, pulled the tape off her mouth and spoke.

"Why did you meet here? Were you expecting anyone else?"

Laura tried to control herself, but the stress was too much for her. Her cheek was burning. For the first time in her life, she was experiencing a genuine fear of dying. She didn't think she could speak. A sound, something like a pathetic croak, came out from the back of her throat. She coughed and tried to say more, but all she could do was gasp. The two men exchanged a look in the mirror, and the blond man tried to reassure her.

"Don't worry; nothing's going to happen to you. We're going to take this guy somewhere. When we get there, we'll set you free, but you need to calm down. OK?"

Laura nodded several times, trying to control herself. Raul was rocking from side to side on the floor. The driver, very aware of the need not to attract attention to his passengers, drove cautiously, respecting all the rules of the road even though they were the only car on the street. Before they got out of the industrial district, they stopped at a red light on a long, straight road flanked by warehouses and empty lots. They were soon joined by a souped-up sports car driven by some neighborhood kids. They started to rev their engine, staring defiantly at the occupants of the Focus. The blond man ignored them, but his companion met their stares. When the lights changed, they pulled away with a squeal and the smell of burning rubber. The driver didn't follow them, and once they'd pulled out in front, the kids stopped to wait for them so their insults could be heard. The man in the back discreetly took a gun from his jacket and lowered the window. The driver didn't move a muscle. He simply sat grave faced, staring ahead. The shouts and catcalls increased in volume. A beer can flew through the air and hit the hood, but he remained unmoved. Then the kids started to reverse slowly until they had halved the distance between the cars. The man in the back got ready with his hand on the doorknob.

In the end, the kids grew tired of them, threw another more poorly directed beer can, and sped away, honking their horn. The two gunmen waited until they'd gone. They hadn't noticed that Raul had squirmed himself next to the door. The car started off, but before it had gotten into second gear, Raul managed to open the door and throw himself into the darkness, rolling down the slope. His captor reached after him in vain, giving him more time to escape. Raul rolled over a few times and then stood up, ignoring the pain from the beating. The car stopped suddenly, and the assassin ran after him with the blond man's recriminations ringing in his ears. The sudden stop threw Laura against the dashboard and then the door, which she desperately tried to open. Before she could get out, the blond man grabbed her shoulder. She tried to pull away with animal desperation, but he had no trouble subduing her. Then her legs took over: she slipped them out onto firm ground while he, hindered by his seat belt, lost his grip. Somehow, Laura got up and started to run into the darkness faster than she'd ever run before. Her temples throbbed, and her chest pounded and burned. She focused on a set of streetlamps in the distance, on the other side of an empty lot. Her nostrils stung, and she squeezed her eyes shut in an effort to go even faster. Her legs felt as though they were being pricked by thousands of needles, and her thighs trembled. As she got to the empty lot, she heard the blond man approaching. He was easily gaining on her. She could feel him eating up yard after yard; he'd almost reached her. But she didn't stop. She couldn't stop. Then, just as she sensed a hand reaching for her, an immense crack rang out; something akin to a thunderclap filled the block, echoing sharply around the empty lot. She was dazed, but she kept going, driven more by momentum than her muscles. She plunged into the darkness, oblivious to the risk of a wrong step or twisted ankle.

The blond man stopped dead. He'd been just about to get her when he heard the shot. His colleague had fired his gun. What the fuck had happened? The junkie couldn't have been that hard to catch. The three people crossing the street on the other side of the lot stopped and turned toward them. He had to let the girl go; she had no idea how lucky she was. She mustn't even have seen them. He had to get back to the car. Then he'd find the idiot who'd fired his gun, waking up half the city as though this were a movie.

Laura went on running and reached the road, where three people were staring at her, dumbfounded. A woman tried to stop her with concern etched all over her face, but she ignored her and went on running and running.

5

Jota was at home watching TV when the buzzer went off. It didn't stop buzzing. Annoyed and a little alarmed, he let in whoever it was without asking questions and went out into the stairwell, ready to bawl them out. But then Laura made her nightmarish entrance. He'd never expected to see her again, and now here she was, trembling all over, stumbling up the stairs, shaking like a leaf, her clothes disheveled, her face swollen and covered in tears and saliva, while her hands were bound with plastic restraints. She had a crazy look in her eyes, the look of someone who'd just escaped death. Then she crumpled onto him and began to sob uncontrollably. All she wanted in the world at that moment was to feel safe. Laura laid her head on Jota's chest, crying. Every time he tried to coax her into the house, she shuddered. She stood stubbornly in the hall, refusing to allow herself to be led, clawing irrationally at his body. Eventually he decided to pick her up to bring the scene in the stairwell to an end.

Once they were inside, he put her down on the sofa and with great effort managed to separate himself so he could get a pair of scissors and cut the restraints. As soon as she was free, she took back some measure of control and went to the bathroom to clean her face. She spent several minutes behind the door, hiding herself away until she felt a little better. Jota was waiting outside, dressed for the street with the car keys and a blanket, shocked into silence. He didn't ask any questions but wrapped her in the blanket and walked her back to the sofa, where he gave her some water, and she slowly calmed down. As she spoke, blood showed on her gums.

"I . . . I didn't know where to go."

"Are you OK? What happened? Who was it? Do we need to go to the hospital?"

"I'm fine—they didn't do anything. Really."

Jota had waited to see what state she was in before picking up the phone.

"What are you doing?"

"Calling the police, of course."

"No! I won't go!"

She got up and clumsily headed for the door.

"Don't go! What's wrong with you? You need to see a doctor. I'm going to call the police and take you to a hospital."

"No, please, don't call. I can't face it right now. Just let me stay for a while. Please, then I'll go."

"We need to go to the hospital. A doctor needs to see you immediately, even if it's just to take some samples."

"I haven't been raped, Jota," Laura said calmly. "I was hit twice in the face, but I escaped before they could do anything else."

Jota looked at the young woman quizzically, wondering if she was frightened enough to lie. "Are you telling the truth? It's very important that we act quickly. I know it's hard."

"I promise. Just let me stay a little while."

"Fine, fine. Tell me what happened, and when you're feeling calmer, we'll go to the police. I'll go with you."

Jota made up the bed in his spare room and made some tea while she spoke, trying to get her ideas in order. She stumbled through an account of what had happened, jumping from one thing to another as each new incident came to mind. Jota listened and took mental notes as he tended to the wounds on her wrists, legs, and face. After a long explanation, when Laura was about to collapse from exhaustion, she got to the start of the tale. For some reason, she'd been working backward.

"You were right. My father sold the clock. After I gave you that paperwork, I heard him talking on the phone several times. He was still trying to get there before you. I think he tried to get it back. He had an appointment the night that he . . . well, when I got to the store, it was wrecked, but I knew that it hadn't been an ordinary robbery."

"Why?"

"He was so nervous. He was afraid of someone. I think that he would have canceled the deal if he could have. I started to visit the people he'd spoken to before the appointment."

"Do you think that the clock has some value, or there's something dangerous about it?"

"I don't know. All I know is that in the last few days, he was trying to keep me away from the store. He didn't want me there."

"Let me tell you what we're going to do. First thing tomorrow, we'll go down to the police station."

"No!"

"Let me finish. I'm not going to make you fill out a report with some illiterate kid. We'll go straight to the captain. Rodrigo, you know him? He knew your father. He's a good friend."

"And what will he do?"

"A lot more than you think. If something crazy really is going on, I trust him more than anyone."

"Oh yeah, what if he talks to your friends in the neighborhood? Someone who knows you? What happens to me?"

"Nothing, so long as you don't do anything else foolish. Nobody asked you to go looking for those thugs."

"So the police are going to handle it?"

"That's how it has to be."

"But I know how your world works. The police have nothing to do with it. Your friend just makes sure you can do your dirty work without being bothered. When did you or my father ever go to the police for anything? You're just sending me to them because you want to get rid of me, because I'm Diego's girl."

"So what do you want to do?"

Suddenly Laura's face clouded over with rage; it was an expression Jota had never seen before. "I want you to kill them."

Jota let her words hang there for a while before saying, "I think you've got the wrong guy."

"I know you know people who can do it."

"You should go ask your boyfriend. I don't do that kind of thing."

"You don't? Or is it just that I'm not my mother?"

Jota gave her a sharp look, then took a deep breath to stop himself from flying off the handle. The girl was in a terrible state. She had the mean-spiritedness of youth, that readiness to say hurtful things. She knew exactly how to drive him crazy, just like her mother used to.

"You don't know what you're talking about."

"You're a cowardly piece of shit, just like my dad. I was wrong to come. You're shitting yourself, just like he used to."

Jota stood up furiously, unable to contain himself any longer. "Who do you think you are? What the hell are you doing here? What does any of this have to do with me? So they killed your dad? It was a long time coming! Get out of here, and go looking for them—maybe you can get yourself killed too. But they won't even do that. The worst that will happen to you is a couple of slaps for getting in the way. Just like last night."

Laura didn't answer. She stayed silent and shrank away, avoiding his gaze. Jota stalked out of the room in frustration. He wandered around the apartment, poured himself a neat gin, and listened, but she didn't make a sound. Another glass later, Jota stood in the doorway and spoke without going inside.

"Tomorrow, I'll get in touch with some people. We won't talk to the cops. We'll do what we always do. I haven't had anything to do with your father for quite some time. You'll need to give me the list of contacts."

Laura looked up at him. Her face was soaking wet, and she had a desperate look in her eye. "They killed him," she whispered, her voice trembling. "They killed my father . . . they killed my daddy."

Jota couldn't get to sleep. He opened his eyes, and for a moment he was scared again. He couldn't identify the fear, but it was crippling, as though he'd never get out of this mess, whatever it was, alive. He sat up in bed and felt the pillow: it was damp with sweat. Then he walked over to the mirror, where only his tired face looked back at him. It was exhausted from years of waiting. Jota lost himself in his own reflection, allowing his gaze to bore straight through him. His eyes slipped out of focus, and soon the reflection became nothing but a blur, darker toward the edges, with two gleaming lights for eyes. He was looking feverish, unhinged. Just like back then. Jota felt the heat rising up his back and once again thought he saw a fire burning behind him. Flames burning up his world, but not his memories. He instinctively lifted his pajama top to look at a scar he hadn't felt in years. The old burned skin, rough and insensitive, was throbbing again.

Jota went back to bed. He lit a cigarette and smoked it without really being aware of what he was doing. He lit a second cigarette, having forgotten that he'd already started one. His restlessness drove him out into the hall, where he went into the living room and poured himself another neat gin. Gin and fear. He tried not to make a sound so as not to wake Laura. He listened closely for any sounds from her bedroom, but it was quiet. At least she was sleeping. Jota began to feel afraid again, but this time it wasn't for himself. He wasn't concerned with his own safety and had no fear of death or pain. A man with nothing to lose was a man without fear. What Jota was feeling was the terror of being responsible for someone; having the girl in his apartment brought back the old tremors. He couldn't be responsible for someone's life, not again. His head pounded with a single name. It hurt like a wound: Laura.

Jota got up before dawn, before his alarm went off. He listened. Everything was still. Laura's door was closed. He made coffee and drank it as he tried to think. He waited until later to call the cleaning lady to tell her not to come in this week, making up a story about how he was working with solvents and the fumes might be dangerous. She chose to believe him.

Laura woke up with a jolt of terrible anxiety that dragged her out of bed. For a few moments she didn't know where she was or what had happened until the memories gradually came flooding back. She realized that this apartment was the only place where she felt safe. Then she went through the several WhatsApp messages the boy had sent her. He was desperately in love with her. She sent a listless reminder: she was back with her mother, and the relationship was over.

Jota weighed his options: in his favor was the fact that there was nothing to tie him to Diego. No one was going to look for Diego's daughter at his apartment or suspect him. Against him was the fact that he couldn't hide her there forever. If Diego really had been killed over the clock, how much danger was he in? Maybe whoever it was knew that he was forging it—that he wasn't a threat. Was he under surveillance? It seemed as though he only had two choices: take Laura to the police right away, and trust them to protect her, or get involved and try to fix things, just like old times. But he wasn't sure that he had the energy. He was burdened by an exhaustion that had built up over many years of denial. *There's always another way*, he reasoned. And right now it seemed the right way to go: he'd find out how much of what the girl was saying was true; find Raul, if he was still alive; and start digging around until he had something to give to the authorities, so long as that wouldn't put her in any more danger. He gave himself five days, maybe a week. After that, he'd give everything he had to Rodrigo and be able to extricate himself from this mess without leaving her in the lurch.

Laura came out of the bedroom with eyes still red from sleep, accumulated exhaustion, and tears. The pain that had eased amid the intense emotions of the night came back now: her face was swollen and burning, and her nose was itchy, as though she was suffering from allergies. She felt undone, physically ravaged, but calmer and safer. They spoke for hours about her ideas, his plans, and how she needed to stay in the apartment for the week. He'd get her some clothes, and they'd have to say something to her uncle. They wouldn't tell her mother anything, just that she'd be back in five days. When the police started the investigation, everything would come out into the open. He should never be mentioned; he couldn't be linked to her. Laura gave him all the information she could remember about the car: a black Ford Focus with a dent in the hood, if they hadn't repaired it already. Jota prepared himself for a quick tour of everywhere he thought he might be able to pick up information. Laura agreed not to go anywhere. For the moment that was sweet relief: she barely had the energy to stand up. Before going out, Jota reminded her that she couldn't talk about this to anyone—her safety depended on it.

"And you won't tell anyone either?" she responded. "Isn't there anyone you trust?"

"It's not a question of trust. It's about discretion."

As he'd expected, Jota couldn't find Raul. He'd disappeared off the face of the earth, and nobody seemed particularly worried about it. But he knew who to talk to, how to spread the word. Raul had been looking for him, and now he couldn't find Raul. He wasn't at his mother's house, but he'd heard that someone had found him somewhere to squat and hide out. The bait had been laid; he just had to wait for someone to bite.

His next stop was the Castillo de Loarre. Mariano was surprised to see him in the morning; he knew without being told that Jota must be looking for something.

"I need your help. For real this time. You know everything that goes on in this neighborhood. I told you about the clock I'm working on for Morgades?"

"I remember."

"Did you know that Diego was trying to muscle in on the deal?"

"Yes, of course. Using Raul. Everyone knew."

"Raul's gone, and I think he wanted to tell me something about the clock."

"He came in talking nonsense the other day."

"What kind of nonsense?"

"I'm sure you know all about it."

"And what do you think?"

"That it's nonsense. And so should you."

"Why?"

"Because it gets people thinking. You threatened Diego over that deal; then you beat up Gabriel for mentioning his daughter. If anyone were to make a list of people who wanted to do Diego harm, you'd be right at the top. I've heard people saying that a few times already. What Raul was saying doesn't help you at all. He was afraid for his life, and after that fight, you were refusing to help him. Everyone's talking about it. You'd better leave it alone for a while, until things calm down. You don't want to get mixed up in it."

"I think that Raul might have been right. I need you to find him as soon as possible. And Diego's girl too. I know what you're going to say, and I don't want to hear it. I think she might know something, and I want to know if she's still around or if she's gone back to her mother."

"I'll do it, but I don't like it one bit."

"Neither do I, but I have no choice. If something really did happen to Diego because of the clock, I could be next. I need to get ahead of this." Jota discreetly slid a piece of paper across the bar to Mariano. "This is a list of the names of people Diego had dealings with over the past month, people I don't know. Any of them might be involved. I need you to find out everything you can about them. Someone might just let something interesting slip."

"It's been a long time since I saw you get so involved in something like this. It worries me. Is this the same thing as twenty-five years ago?"

"Yes."

"As I recall, that didn't end too well."

"I know."

After leaving the bar, Jota went to see Richard at his gym and then Adolfo at the store. He gave each a slightly different version of the story, testing for leaks. He asked Richard about a blond man with a black Ford Focus that Raul had told him about; he might be a hit man, and he might not be alone. With Adolfo, he only asked after Raul. But he asked everyone where Laura might be. Letting it be known that he was looking for her was the only way to be sure that they wouldn't find her. He wouldn't ask anyone else. Those were the only three people he trusted, and even so he had laid traps for each. It was the life they lived. On his way to see Morgades, his blood started to pump without his realizing it. He was feeling more alive than he had in years. The fire had never gone out completely. His adrenaline had begun to take over.

Morgades's secretary led him to the office door to announce the visit. Jota went in grave faced.

She met him warmly. "I got your messages. I've been monitoring your progress: you know where the piece came from, the first seller in Madrid, and you're very close to finding it. I can't say that I'm surprised, but allow me to say how happy I am. Why hide it? I'm anxious to find out why you wanted to meet. Have you brought me something to brighten my day?"

"On this occasion, I'm going to have to disappoint you. I'll certainly have the piece in the next few weeks, but there have been one or two hiccups."

Morgades's expression turned sour. "What kind of hiccups? Is this about money? Because if so, nothing doing. I've already agreed to pay you too much, and you've had your advance payment."

"It doesn't have anything to do with money. I think that your client is hiding information from the both of us. Or maybe you are."

Jota stared hard at Morgades, but all he saw was suspicion, which was only to be expected.

"I've shared everything I know."

"Then maybe I should meet your client."

"What? Have you gone mad? You know that's impossible. Why would I share my client with you? What about my cut?"

"I didn't think you'd like that. Then tell me what you've been hiding."

The tension steadily increased as Morgades held his stare. "I haven't hidden anything from you."

"I know that someone has offered to get you the clock behind my back."

Suddenly Morgades relaxed. "You want to get in touch with my client because you think that I've been dealing with someone behind your back?"

"That's right."

Morgades spread her arms like a peacock does its plumage, and Jota knew that he'd made a mistake. It was obvious that Morgades had nothing to fear; she wasn't doing any deals behind his back. He'd just served himself up on a silver platter.

"I'm surprised by you, Jota. I would never have expected such a cheap trick. Do you know what I think? I don't think you have anything, and you'd like to swindle me, but it'd be even easier to swindle my client. They'll buy whatever you have to say, and I'll be out of the picture. No, my friend, I'm not going to play that little game. And I'll tell you something else: I haven't dealt with anyone else, but if I do, I'd be well within my rights. The only person I have to answer to is my client, and if anyone offers me the same piece for cheaper, be under no illusion that I won't take it. It's your job to find it, not mine. But I'd at least call you to let you know—that's the difference between us. I have no intention of letting you talk to my client."

Jota tried to repair the damage. He'd lost any hope of getting in touch with the client. He wondered how he could have made such a stupid mistake. "Forget your client. Do you know Diego Blanco?"

"Who? No."

"He was a former partner of mine."

"And what does he have to do with this?"

"I heard that he'd started to look for the clock. If he'd have found it before me, he'd have offered it to you. Maybe he never got in touch."

"If he's involved, I have no problem doing a deal with the both of you."

"Something's happened to him."

Morgades showed no surprise; she wasn't the kind to be easily shocked. "What? Was it you?"

"No. I think someone doesn't want us looking for the clock. They don't want us to find it. That's why I think your client knows something we don't. Whoever it is, I need an explanation, and I don't care who it comes from."

"What you're saying is very serious."

"Now try to reconsider. Why would I go to your client to swindle them when you know very well that they'd call you five minutes after I'd left?"

Morgades thought about this. She tried to read Jota's expression; he didn't seem to be lying. Jota saw that he'd rattled her, although her tone sounded more confident. But he still didn't understand his mistake. What was he missing?

"Fine, I'll call them. Leave me alone. My secretary will see to you."

Jota sat in the large anteroom, opposite the secretary's desk.

"Would you like a coffee?"

"No, thank you."

Then he thought again. "Actually, yes I would. I don't know how long I'll have to wait."

The secretary gave him a polite smile before heading out to a kitchenette to the side. While he was gone, Jota opened the planner on the desk and scanned it for dates, appointments, and names until he heard footsteps approaching. He sat back down. It was a long while before Morgades called him back in. She apologized for the wait but said the conversation had been difficult. She looked tired.

"The deal's off."

"What?"

"Maybe you're right, maybe not—I don't know. My client says that they have no idea if the clock, or anything else in the lot, has a secret worth they don't know about, but they were scared by what I had to say. They don't want any trouble, so they've canceled the commission."

"But they can't do that! You know I'm about to find it; I'm almost there. I've put a lot into this, using my own money. I need to talk to the client. We can't leave things like this."

"The deal hasn't changed. The advance covers any costs you might have incurred. It was you who came to my office with crazy stories. What did you expect my client to do? You might have lost out on this one job, but do you know what I've lost?"

"Give me your client's name."

"You know I won't do that. Especially not now."

They both sat in silence for a moment. Jota decided to be on his way. He knew that the client knew the real value of the clock but probably not who was trying to keep it from them. Otherwise they wouldn't have been trying to look for it. Now Jota didn't care about the clock.

Laura spent the majority of her day thinking, fantasizing, and obsessing and then, having exhausted herself, trying to rest. She let her mind run a mile a minute; it didn't seem to want to switch off. Only occasionally did Laura manage to shake herself out of it, watching TV and sleeping at irregular intervals. As evening approached, an abstract anguish fell upon her again. She found herself sitting on the floor in the bathroom, leaning against the sink, staring at a tile that reflected some of her hair, counting each strand. She was still fiddling with the pen, getting tenser and tenser, lost in unreal thoughts. A couple of hours earlier, the cat had appeared out of nowhere, and now it was studying her curiously, unafraid, staying at a prudent distance but without hiding. She'd barely noticed it. When she heard the door opening, Laura watched the cat head toward the sound. Then she heard it hiss in the hall and the sound of Jota swearing. It streaked back across her line of vision, heading for its hiding place. When she heard Jota, Laura came back to the real world, her soul revived. She got up and tried to make herself look normal.

"Hello! Are you hungry? I made a pasta salad. How was your day? Did you find anything out?"

"No, it's still too soon to expect anything. How's your face?"

"Well, it doesn't hurt anymore. It's annoying though; my eye was throbbing this morning. It was horrible, but it's stopped now."

"It doesn't seem serious, but maybe you should see a doctor."

"What are you planning to do with me?"

"I don't know."

Jota collapsed onto the sofa. He was acting strange, distant, lost in thought.

"What's wrong?"

"It's been a long day."

For a moment she was afraid, but she didn't know of what—maybe being left alone or losing his trust. Or perhaps she was just afraid of going outside.

"You don't believe me, do you? You haven't found any evidence, and you're worried about me staying here."

"Yes, I am worried. But I believe you."

"If you talk to your friend Raul, I'm sure that—"

"I won't be able to talk to him. Rodrigo just called. He wanted me to come to his office right away, but I've put him off until tomorrow morning so I can think about what to do with you."

"Is he dead?"

"Apparently."

"Raul knew they were looking for him."

"So?"

"What about me?"

"That's the question. We should go to see Rodrigo. They can protect you better than I can."

"So why don't I just go now and leave you in peace? Call the police. I'll report the attack, and you'll never see me again."

"You don't understand. These people are professional killers. I can't protect you from them. If I talk to Rodrigo tomorrow, it'll be different from filing a report. He can take care of you right away. You'll be safe."

"What if you're wrong? He's your friend, but he doesn't know me. What's he going to do to protect me? Nobody knows that I'm here."

"For now," Jota said. "I need to think things through. For the moment take this. It's not much, but you should take it anyway." Jota handed her a small cylinder not much larger than a tube of lipstick. "Pepper spray. You won't need it here, but keep it in your bag. If you ever have to use it, it'll give you time to get away, no more than that. I'll feel better knowing you have it."

Laura thanked him, but she had no idea what to do with it. They spoke some more about unimportant things, shared ideas, learning how to relax and be in the same space together. Time passed slowly, and Jota knew that the sense of calm this girl induced in him would last only a few days. It was a mirage, but he couldn't resist it. He knew that he wouldn't tell Rodrigo about her, and maybe the real reason for that had nothing to do with her at all. Maybe he was being selfish in wanting to keep her close by.

The next morning Jota went to meet Rodrigo at his office. Rodrigo didn't greet Jota as he came in but let him sit down in silence, his usual tactic. Jota knew it well. Neither of them spoke. Where many of those who were invited into this office would have been unnerved, it just told Jota that this wasn't a friendly invitation. He'd need to stay on his toes. After a lengthy period of artificial tension, he spoke.

"So what?"

"Tell me that this has nothing to do with you."

"This has nothing to do with me."

"I want you to tell me that this has nothing to do with you, and I want it to be true."

"Fuck, it's true. I came to hear what you had to say."

"Why did you visit Diego?"

"I thought you'd called me as a friend, not to interrogate me."

"So why aren't you answering me like a friend?"

"Because I have nothing to say to the police captain. If this is a formal interrogation, we both know that there are proper channels."

"So tell me that you're not hiding anything."

"You know that I hide things, but they have nothing to do with your investigation. I'm saying that as a friend."

Rodrigo went silent again. Jota could sense how agitated he was. Rodrigo knew Jota's limits, and he wasn't going to violate them. In the end, he was the first to put his cards on the table.

"It's an organized group, Jota. Raul and Diego were killed by the same gang. They're professionals. You know that as well as I do."

"You're wrong. I don't know anything."

"I can include your name in my report to the prosecutor. With your record, they'll question you."

"You don't scare me. I paid my dues a long time ago. I don't have anything to worry about."

"This is serious. I don't know what's going on or who else might be at risk, but they're not done yet. You need to keep me in the loop. This is me asking, not the police captain."

"Are you going to stop them? Will they be arrested?"

"Who? I need you to help me."

"I'll say it again. I don't know anything, and that's true. You just told me that it's a gang."

"It might be the Mafia, or maybe they're hired killers. All I know is that you had some trouble with Diego just before all this began."

"Diego was trying to muscle in on a commission. He went through Raul, and I went to warn him off. But that doesn't mean anything. He used the junkie for all his dirty tricks; it was just business as usual."

"What was your commission?"

"I'll happily give you the information, client included. It was an ordinary recovery job. It's just an unfortunate coincidence. I didn't see Diego or Raul again. If it had something to do with my job, they'd have got rid of me too."

"But you're a survivor."

"You think too much of me."

"How much are you hiding?"

"Enough for my purposes, nothing of use to you."

Rodrigo stood up and stared at him, hard. Jota knew that he was the police captain again. The fragile balance between them was maintained.

"I don't want your name to come up again, not while this case is open."

"Neither do I, I can assure you."

Jota gave Rodrigo Morgades's contact information. He thought the shock of a visit from the police was perfect payback for her screwing up the deal. Rodrigo and his men's intrusion into her sacrosanct space would be most unwelcome. And she'd have to give them her client's name. If there was any joy to be had down that path, Rodrigo would find it, and Jota knew that he'd share it with him.

After leaving the police station, Jota headed straight for Raul's apartment. He knew that they'd be getting a warrant to search it, if they hadn't already, and he chided himself for not going as soon as he heard the news. He was being slow and clumsy. He was out of practice. His instincts weren't as sharp as they used to be, and now he'd wasted valuable time. He'd missed obvious clues about what was happening and maybe who was behind it all. Jota felt like an amateur, and any consequences of that would be on his head. It wasn't just this: he'd crossed a line, and now he'd need a long-term strategy to cover himself. Who might want him dead? The fire gleamed in the darkness. Jota was afraid to get any closer, but something inside him had been awakened. He was attracted to the flames like a moth heading for its own destruction.

He rang the doorbell for several minutes, but no one came to open up. He could hear clearly that the television was on, but he knew that Raul's mother wasn't getting up. He kept on ringing until he finally heard her stand and move toward the door. She opened it and looked out, but he realized that she wasn't seeing him. Her face was dirty, her eyes sticky with sleep, and she was in a nightgown. He'd never seen her like that. Doña Asunción had endured a life of tragedy; her dignity had been her only defense. Her alcoholic husband had left her several times, but she'd supported him, working as a cleaning lady until he'd left for good. Drugs had already taken one of her sons; Raul, the younger one, had been hooked and headed toward the same fate until she'd intervened. She, along with Raul's innate instinct for survival, had gotten him through it, and he'd stayed to keep her company, giving her all the love he was capable of. She'd endured all this with great dignity and stoicism; her home had always been neat and tidy, and she'd always been ready for company even if she spent most of her time alone in front of the television. She'd always been a lady, even when her son stole her appliances to sell, but now she'd given up. Doña Asunción was like a ghost who'd lost touch with reality. Once the door was open, she went back to the television without a word. Jota said hello, and she nodded a few times, as though to show that she knew he was there. Maybe even thanking him for coming. She must have been the first to get the news, perhaps days ago, perhaps on the very night that Laura had come to see him. After all these years struggling against the pain and misery, Doña Asunción had lost the battle. She'd given up.

"Why are you on your own?" he asked. *How could they have left her alone?* he wondered. The neighborhood women may have mocked her behind her back because of her sons, but they'd always come to visit. Now they'd abandoned her. *This is a bestial society*, Jota thought. *They've left her alone because they know that she's going to die.* "Don't you have any family you can visit? You need to get out of here."

She looked up gratefully and smiled with resignation. It was what she'd been taught ever since she was a girl: to be resigned to her fate. Women of her generation had been led down the path of docility, and now here she was, about to lose everything. Jota found himself cleaning up dirty dishes, taking her to the bathroom to wash her face, and pushing her into the bedroom to get dressed. When she came back out, she looked just as bereft but a little more human. There was nothing else Jota could do; he'd leave, and she'd sit back down and let herself crumble away. He felt impotent.

"I need to look through Raul's things."

The woman didn't say a word, but she nodded at everything he said, her eyes still on the TV program, as though it would back her up. The apartment was dark, small, and very depressing. He went into Raul's bedroom. The bed was unmade and covered in magazines and detritus, as though he'd only just left. Jota inspected everything he found—loose pieces of paper, half-empty address books, a couple of folders—but there was nothing useful. He went back into the living room.

"I'll find them, Doña Asunción. I'll find the people who did it."

Raul's mother suddenly seemed to perk up. She turned to him. Her voice was dull and neutral. "And what good would that do?"

Before continuing his sleuthing, Jota allowed himself a break to deal with some unfinished business. After a long journey he got to the old man's watch shop. His elderly friend was beaming. Jota chuckled at his bad luck.

"Tell me that for the first time in your life, you're late."

The old man turned around to pick up something, maintaining his smile. "Ha ha. Here it is . . . you'll see . . . we're very happy with this. I told you that I had something special. We've done some great work. It's going to be more expensive, but you won't regret it."

The clock looked exactly as it had in the photograph: the embossed maker's mark, the faded coloring, the rust. The gentleman motioned to him to be quiet for a moment and pointed, cupping his ear: the movement was emitting the sonorous ticktock of a century-old clock. It almost certainly ran slow, just as it should. He looked at Jota with glee, genuinely proud of his work.

Adolfo seemed amused by the turn of events, even though it meant losing his share. The work had been incredible. The old man hadn't duplicated a movement so perfectly in years; even a seasoned professional would have accepted it without a second glance. In spite of everything, he tried to look on the bright side: the challenge had invigorated everyone. They'd been lying dormant for too long. Jota thought this was all very well, but he no longer cared about the clock. He'd broken even on the deal, and now his thoughts strayed elsewhere.

After he examined the piece, Adolfo's voice grew grave. "So Raul's gone."

"I went to see his mother. She's lost her mind."

"She's had to put up with too much in her life."

"I didn't find anything."

"That was only to be expected. The neighborhood's in uproar; people are nervous."

"It seems that someone's poked a hornet's nest."

"Yeah, and you're sitting too close to the action. As usual."

"Are you going to lecture me too?"

"No, but this isn't a game anymore. What is there for us to gain? Why go on asking questions? You won't get to sell it, and Diego isn't going to steal anything from you now. Neither is poor Raul."

"I don't know what's at stake. Or whether I'll be next. That's reason enough."

"I know all this reminds you of what happened before. For me, too, and that's what worries me. We're not the men we were, Jota, and we haven't got any more years to waste. I have a family and two daughters who depend on me. I can't be following you everywhere you want to go."

Jota noticed a slight tic from his friend, which worried him. "How are things with Miriam?"

"Well . . . you know how it is. She's been irritable the past few days. I need to spend more time with her and the kids. This isn't what we do anymore, Jota."

"No, it's not like it was back then. Not even close. But this time I need to get to the bottom of it, whatever it takes. You can walk away if you want."

"Of course that's what I want, but you know I won't. Raul was hiding in an empty house on Calle Olvidados. It wasn't hard to get that information. If they really were looking for him, I can't understand why it took them so long."

"Have you been to see it?"

"No, I thought it might be a good idea to see Pup, Raul's friend, first. He found it for him. He must know something."

"Know something that he'll gladly sell. I'll go see him. Are you going to search the apartment?"

"Either this afternoon or early tomorrow morning."

At lunchtime, the streets started to empty. Pup was dressed in the kinky but shabby style of the 1980s. His body was covered in scars and tattoos, and one of his arms was in a sling. He was headed out of the park, on his way home. He slipped into an alley in his habitual furtive manner and bumped into an unsmiling Jota.

"Hello, Pup. What a surprise. On your way to lunch?"

"N-no. Listen, I'm in a hurry."

Jota wasn't in the mood to waste time. He grabbed Pup's arm and twisted it without even looking at him. The man howled in pain.

"So am I. So tell me who you sold out Raul to, and I'll leave you alone."

"Ow! Ooooowww! I don't know anything—I promise!"

"You knew I was coming, or else you wouldn't have been acting so shifty."

He pushed Pup to the ground and pulled his arm behind his back. There was a slight click, and the man started to scream.

"Ooow! Aaaaaaah! No, no, no, no! Raul asked me to hide him, so I took him somewhere, but they must have followed him. A man came to see me. He was bad—he looked like a bastard. He was blond, very big. I told him that I didn't know what he was talking about, and he broke my fingers. Please stop—it hurts. I had to tell him where Raul was, but he didn't care because they knew that. He said that if he got away, if they lost him even for a second, he'd kill me on the spot. It was my job to make sure that he didn't escape. And that was it. I never saw him again. He just told me to make sure that Raul slept there, and the night he went missing, I was scared because I thought he'd escaped without my noticing, and they'd kill me. But then, when they found him, I realized that they'd killed him. I never saw him again. I promise that's all I know."

"You didn't see their car, anything out of the ordinary? Nothing else you want to tell me?"

"I don't know. He had a black Ford Focus; that's all I know. Nothing else, I swear. Let me go, please—it hurts."

Jota let up, satisfied that Pup had nothing left to say. Another poor bastard who'd sold out a guy who was supposedly his friend. He didn't even have the decency to feel guilty about it, preoccupied as he was by his own mangy survival. That had been Raul's world, the life they lived.

Jota returned to his apartment with the clock, which he'd already forgotten about. His head was filled with unanswered questions: If they knew where he was, why not kill Raul beforehand? Why wait for Laura when she had nothing to do with it? They were looking for someone else, and they had expected to find them that night. But he was the only one who might have gone. Unless there was someone else, someone who'd been warned and was in hiding. For the moment it didn't matter; it was just useless speculation. He was groping around in the dark.

Laura was both curious about and repelled by the clock. At first it made her feel physically sick to see it, and she started to gag as though it were a festering wound on her father's body. Then she began to admire Jota's skill as a forger. Aware of her fragile state, he managed to distract her with a quick account of how he'd done it. The clock continued its weary ticktock on the table as Jota's face was lost in a cloud of cigarette smoke.

"It looks just the same as the photo. But what good is it to you now?"

"Yesterday it was worth eight thousand euros; now I don't know."

Laura giggled a little for the first time in what felt like a long time. "I'm sorry—do you mind me laughing?"

He shrugged and took a long drag on his cigarette.

"I know how much you've done for me over the past few days. I want to thank you. I acted like an idiot when I first arrived. I'm sorry for reacting like that when you said you were going to call the police. I ruined your deal."

"That's yet to be seen."

"No. I was thinking about what you said. I was hoping things would be different. I . . . I always dreamed that you'd take me on an adventure one day."

"An adventure?"

"Do you remember when I said I loved coming to your house? My dad always acted like an old man. Even when I was little and he was still young. He was always hanging around with old people obsessed with dusty old relics, people who lived surrounded by ancient furniture or in cellars, spending weeks without seeing the sunlight. Then I realized that they were afraid of life—it was why they locked themselves away. My father did that."

"So did I."

"No, you were different. You came and went; you fooled them; you cheated them. You were always on your way somewhere else, running from one thing to another, because you always had something more interesting to do. You were great . . ."

"Or so you thought."

"I don't remember being happy as a child. My mother never loved my father. Ever since I can remember, she looked down on him. When you're little, that's all you know; you have nothing to compare it to. I thought that was what parents were like, that was what families were like. Then you grow up and realize that it's all bullshit. They had no right to make me live like that. Our home was claustrophobic, so I dreamed of you. I dreamed of excitement, travel, adventures, and that one day I'd run away with you. You'd rescue me from my father's store and take me to strange new places, on missions and stuff. We'd go to exotic countries with jungles, sunlight . . . a lot of sunlight, like on TV."

"You've got to be kidding."

"I'm not! To me, you were like Indiana Jones. A cross between Indiana Jones and Boromir from *Lord of the Rings*."

"The handsome one?"

"No, the one that dies. But in a superbrave way. I was just a little girl, and you had that worn-out jacket."

"Fuck, that leather jacket."

"Yeah, you see? I remember it perfectly. I thought you looked just like them."

"Why, thank you."

"I think I was still thinking a little like that when all this began. I think I was secretly dreaming about that adventure. But you've done so much more. You've done more than I can ever repay. So . . . so much. I really do admire you."

"You've only spent a couple of days in my apartment. Don't go overboard."

"I'm not!" Laura insisted, looking around as if something had changed. "Do you still have the jacket?"

"That old one? It must be around here somewhere."

"Get it out, please."

"What? I haven't worn it in . . . well, I don't know how long it's been."

"Get it out, really."

"You want me to put it on?"

"Yes, yes please!"

Jota took some persuading to make a fool of himself, but then he remembered that the girl had lost her father just a few days ago. Also, her whole life she'd been paying for all their youthful mistakes. Mistakes whose consequences you so often passed on to the little people who depended on you the most, children incapable of judging before it was too late. Jota went to look for his fraudulent hero's jacket, if only to repay her a little with what he had on hand, a little joy and laughter.

Jota knew something definitive was brewing when he got an early-morning message to call on Mariano at the Castillo de Loarre. He waited for the office workers to finish their breakfast and then went to speak to him.

"That was fast."

"It wasn't hard. After what happened to your friend Raul, everything's gone to hell. It's strange—a lot's coming to light, as though it's about more than just your mess. People are drinking and talking a lot more."

"About what?"

"About things that have nothing to do with us. Things we thought had been forgotten. And a lot about you."

"So I've been declared guilty? I've heard that one already."

"No one says it out loud, but they've been putting things together: Diego, Gabi, Rafa's assistant, Raul . . ."

"Fuck Gabriel. That had nothing to do with it."

"No, but you beat him up. You went crazy, and everyone saw you. They all knew it was about Diego's daughter. Then you come in here asking about her."

Jota smiled in satisfaction. Mariano interpreted this as defiance, brazenness in the face of the danger he was in, the trouble that was coming his way and everyone who was behind it.

"So what have you been able to find out?" Jota asked.

"Some say that she went back to her mother, others that she went to the beach with some friends. All I know is that she's not here, and the way things are looking, that's better for everyone, you especially."

"This has nothing to do with her."

"But she comes up a lot. She's Laura's daughter. People aren't stupid."

"All I care about is the clock. That's where the answers are."

"I don't know what answers you're looking for, Jota."

"For now, anything you might have."

"People are talking, but there's nothing very clear cut. Everyone pretty much knew who Diego had dealings with, people from other stores. He was more out of his depth in this than you. The strange thing is that he wasn't working with Rafa. If he wasn't with him or you, maybe he had another scout?"

"Barely anyone does anymore."

"But Diego was old school. How was he going to steal that deal without a scout? You know that he had to have one."

"So was he working with a scout or not?"

"It would seem so. It wasn't too hard to find him: a contact who's come up again and again in recent weeks, someone called Xavi. We don't know him, and now he's disappeared without a trace. It seems that he worked occasionally in our circles, and everyone who's had dealings with him speaks well of him, but he must do other things too. I don't know. He lives in a commuter town to the south. That must be why he only comes occasionally, but I know that since what happened to Diego, no one has seen him around here. It's not unusual, but it sticks out."

"That doesn't tell me much."

"Come on—a scout from outside who barely works with anyone? Who Diego made more calls to over the last month than anyone else? Just when he was trying to screw you over? And after he was killed, no one ever saw him again. I can't give you a signed confession, but I think it's enough for you to go on."

Jota tried to take in the implications of Mariano's information. "Fine. Is there any way to contact him?"

"The telephone number is on the list. I don't know the address, but I have something better. Felix was one of the three dealers who worked with him. I know him well enough to ask, but he hadn't seen Xavi in years and doesn't know anything, although he said good things about him. I don't know the other two, but—and this is what I wanted to tell you—one was on the list you gave me of Diego's contacts."

"That's too much of a coincidence."

"Exactly. Now you know what I'm saying. I think I have your man. Maybe two men."

Jota spent the rest of the morning walking around Retiro Park as though he had all the time in the world and the information he'd just received didn't matter to him at all. Smoking and walking, he stopped for a beer and looked up at the trees, watching the foliage opening and closing like a giant puzzle. This was how he had to be: calm and unhurried. He needed to put his thoughts in order and get his strategy straight, knowing that he couldn't share it with anyone. Somehow he was both scared and relieved about what he had to do. In his mind and soul, the fire was burning. A fire that hadn't stopped for twenty years, even if he'd thought it long since extinguished. But the fire would never stop. It crept on slowly, in silence, burning everything in its path. It burned inside of him, consuming every pore of his skin. As he moved on, he knew that was how it had to be. There was no other way, and he was grateful.

The building was crumbling into the empty lot next door. It had been shored up by metal struts, but there was no guarantee of how long they'd last: a temporary solution to bide time before the structure was declared unfit for use and demolished. It was just a matter of doing the paperwork. As a historic building, it should, and could, have been saved, but the disinterest of the institutions that specialized in such matters had signed its death warrant. What had once been one of the area's traditional housing blocks, a building that had appeared in books and several films in the 1960s, was sagging over, on the verge of collapse. Half of the residences were uninhabited. Doors had been left open or in some cases had disappeared entirely. With its gaping doorways as missing teeth, it looked like the head of a huge moribund animal drying and shrinking in the sun. The stairs were irregular, as in all those old buildings, and had grown slippery. The wood oozed slime, and different materials had come to stick to them over the years to form a dark layer that peeled away at the sides. Parts of the banister had rotted away, making the climb dangerous. In several places, the police tape placed to indicate a dangerous section had come away.

Adolfo walked down the first floor hallway with the confidence of someone who knew where they were going. A hairless old woman locked herself in the bathroom at the end of the corridor when she saw him approaching. Ignoring her, Adolfo went into the apartment Jota had told him to go to and found that it was empty. Piles of dirt had accumulated in every corner, and paint flaked from the walls onto the floor, but he didn't find the dirty clothes he'd been expecting or the kind of filthy mattress or damp sports bags you tended to see in places like these. In fact, he didn't find anything. The plumbing and electricity had long since ceased to function, and the switches and fixtures were gone, which was normal. What he couldn't understand was the lack of trash. He had been planning to search through it for anything that Raul might have left behind, a scrap of paper with a clue, a telephone number, or whatever. He went back out into the hallway and peered into another apartment but found the same thing. Not one for paranoia, he dismissed the idea of someone having gotten here before him and, after thinking for a little while, headed confidently to an apartment on the floor below. Inside, he heard a murmur that disappeared when he knocked on the splintered wooden door, which was locked with a chain where the lock should have been.

"Bobo, open up. It's me!"

He heard the chain being pulled back, and a bald, toothless old man appeared before him with soup-stained lips. Behind him, next to a covered window, a pair of old women peered at him fearfully, sitting on a cot next to a gas burner they used for both heating and cooking. A metal pan had been placed on top of it. Around them were piles of all manner of garbage, and the air was so thick with the stench that it was hard to breathe. Adolfo told himself that Jota was counting on him, and—after chatting to Bobo, giving him his pack of tobacco, and flirting with the two old women, who lit up like schoolgirls—he tried to find out where they'd put the stuff they'd taken from the apartment upstairs, or all the apartments, assuming that there was some method to their hoarder madness. Fortunately for him, there was, and his journey through the strange labyrinth of garbage didn't take as long as he'd feared, although it was still almost more than he could bear. He found Raul's old backpack and even the plastic bag he'd carried on his last visit trying to sell the obscene Lladró figurine. But just as Adolfo had expected, there was nothing helpful. Considering the pointlessness of his trip and how the old folks might get upset at him for stealing their treasures, he left it all, giving them a few euros in thanks, along with a friendly goodbye.

When he got back out onto the street, he heard a woman's voice.

"Are you going to report him?"

He looked up in confusion. The woman was calling from the building opposite, out of a small window in the wall facing the condemned building. Her obese form got as close as it could to the window, but her head was bigger than the frame itself.

"Did you see him, madam?"

"Of course. I see everyone. Oh, I've seen things."

"May I come up?"

"Oh no, dear, I can't let you in my house. It's not a mess like those thieves . . ."

"What?"

Another woman appeared in a second larger window with a better view. She had to crane her neck to talk to him but obviously didn't mind.

"Are you from the TV? It's about time you came to show people what's going on here."

"Shut up—he's talking to me!"

"Don't listen to her; she's a slob. That's why she doesn't want you to see her house! You can come up and film mine if you like. It's always neat and tidy."

"The only slob around here is your daughter!"

"I'm sorry. I don't work for a television show. Did you see the man who was here a couple of nights ago? The one they killed—you must have heard about it."

But now that his media connections had gone up in smoke, the women had lost interest in him and were insulting each other as energetically as they could. But then a large man with a moustache, a dirty shirt, and an East European accent appeared behind Adolfo.

"Are you a journalist?"

The women noticed him and redirected their ire.

"Scum! He's one of the ones they need to get rid of—nothing but scum!"

"No, there's been a misunderstanding. I'm not a journalist."

"They throw garbage out of their windows to get rid of us. I live here with my wife. Why don't you come see?"

The women began to shout even more excitedly, trying to drown out the man.

"Tell him, tell him about the drug addicts and the Africans at night! They shit right down there below us!"

"It's not our fault! We live here, and they're trying to get rid of us!"

More people started to emerge, and there was shouting on all sides, making for a sadly chaotic scene. Adolfo tried to slip away. Now the street was filled with screaming people complaining about crime, poverty, and filth, all expressing their fear of the other, looking for someone to blame it on.

Adolfo walked away, annoyed at having been partly to blame for a stupid fight and even more so at having had to witness it. All he could think about was getting the stink of the apartment out of his nostrils and the shrieking out of his ears. But he had no idea that he'd called attention to himself. Just as Rodrigo had warned Jota, they were dealing with highly trained professionals, and even though they'd dispatched Raul, they weren't going to leave the area unwatched. A simple payment to a kid who worked at the bar opposite to report anything out of the ordinary or any unusual visitors was all it took. Adolfo had managed to get in and out without anyone noticing, but now that he was in the middle of all this commotion, the fact that he'd shown interest in the dead man, Adolfo's description and license plate number would soon be given to someone willing to pay a generous tip for the information. A few hours later, after he called Jota, they met up. Adolfo had little to report other than the fact that the neighborhood was a powder keg. Jota listened closely.

"Fine, we knew that we weren't likely to find anything there, but thanks anyway. Now I need another favor."

"You know what? I'm liking this business less and less. I know that nothing's happened yet, but I'm worried. Maybe because nothing's happened."

"I feel the same way. It's like a pot that's about to boil over."

"Yeah, something like that."

"Then we'd better get the lid off quick."

Jota came out of their meeting sure of his friend's support, but he knew that he was running out of options. He had no idea how long any of his friends would stay with him, and he didn't blame them. Neither did he know how long he should keep going. He didn't need anyone to tell him that he was crossing a dangerous line, maybe a point of no return.

After exploring every corner of Jota's enormous apartment, which was packed full of furniture and intriguing nooks and crannies, Laura thought she'd found something interesting behind an imposing bookcase that didn't seem to fit properly against the wall. After pushing it back with less effort than she'd expected—the case had been placed on top of dishcloths to make it easier to move—she found a small window that looked out onto the roofs of the neighboring buildings. A window covered up by a bookcase but that, surprisingly, was kept open. She tried to close it but found that the window was being kept open on purpose so that the cat Jota refused to admit to owning could come and go as he pleased. They might greet each other with hisses and swear words, but the feline spent more time at home than Jota. Then Laura was shocked to discover bowls of food and water, also behind the bookcase. Had it always been there, or had he moved it just so he could deny that he had a cat?

Later, Laura and the cat were dozing on the sofa, the cat purring on top of her as she stroked his back. Whenever she started to fall asleep and her hand went limp, he'd bat her face until she woke up again. They lay like that for an indeterminate period of time until, as usual, he heard Jota's approach and stretched before running to the door to confront him.

Laura had prepared what she wanted to say. She was well aware of the limbo she was in and was determined to leave. After their conversation the night before, she had been able to think clearly, properly, about where Jota was heading and her plight. Here she was, locked away, a prisoner of her fear, unable to walk away from a game that she'd dragged him into as well. Laura had decided that she would seek help from the police and tell them everything she knew. Then she'd call her mother and go to be with her. She'd say goodbye to her uncle and forget everything. If Jota thought it was safe, she'd let Rodrigo protect her and bring this sorry chapter to an end once and for all. If he said it was dangerous, she'd take responsibility for herself. She wouldn't hide behind him anymore. But when he told her about the progress he'd made, she started to brighten up. He told her about a couple of possible contacts, one of them in an antiques shop that his partner would visit under a pretext. After that, he'd go in himself to get information about someone who he thought held at least some of the answers.

"When you say *go in*, you mean break in, don't you?"

"Call it what you like."

"Do you know it?"

"No, given the location, it won't be very fancy."

When she heard where it was, Laura decided to save her speech for another time. Maybe in twenty-four hours, maybe after escaping the apartment to go see the man that Jota had mentioned. He may not know him, but she did. As soon as she heard the address, she recognized the shop belonging to the old man who'd urged her to walk away. He'd been so nice, and it irritated her that he'd played her for a fool, making her think that her suspicions were just paranoia, that there was no reason to keep investigating. That fucking old man knew the whole story, but he'd treated her like a little girl. And that was how Laura now saw herself, like a little girl whom no one ever told anything. She was furious with him but even more so with herself. While Jota calmly told her about his progress and plans, Laura was thinking about where she might find another set of keys and how to slip out of the apartment without Jota noticing. She tried to calculate how long it would take to get to the mysterious old man and persuade him to tell her the truth. She had to make sure that she wouldn't be recognized on the way.

For some reason the girls didn't have to go to school, but he couldn't remember why. He found them at home after coming back from the shop Jota had asked him to visit. Miriam had left them there to go shopping, allowing herself one of the absences that were becoming longer and more frequent, living a life that she had kept hidden from him for some time now. The girls, completely oblivious, were running around after each other, fighting over an old mask from the civil war that they used to dress up as a monster. He sighed, trying to repress another scolding like the one he'd given them a little while ago. He'd had enough drama for one day. He called Jota to tell him what he'd found out.

"I think this is your guy. I'm almost sure of it. First I asked about a clock, any old one, to see if he'd try to lead me where we want him to go, but the old man's clever, the kind that never leaves the house but knows everything that goes on in the neighborhood."

"Did you get anything out of him?"

"Nothing. He doesn't want anything to do with commissions and didn't even want to look at the photos. He says he can barely see anymore. What a wily old bastard! He was pretty nervous, defensive; he saw through me right from the start."

"Fine."

"Just to make sure, I insisted pretty hard. I took out the photo of the clock. His expression didn't change, but there was a gleam in his eye—you know the kind. It's him, no doubt about it. Are you going to pay him a visit? He's old, but he looks stubborn."

"No, I won't get anything out of him. I'm going to break in tonight. His files will tell me much more than he will. I'll speak to Richard."

"I thought so. I checked out the store: no alarm, door with a simple lock, a metal shutter. I think the storage room is in the basement, so I don't think there's a back door. The shop window has blinds locked up with a chain—that's the best way in."

"Yeah, metal shutters are too noisy. I need to get hold of a cold chisel and the other tools. Good work. Thank you."

"Good luck."

The girls ran into the back while a customer appeared at the door. Adolfo turned toward him. "Good morning. Can I help you?"

The man fixed him with an unsettling stare. He was large and blond and whistled off key as he walked, as though he couldn't remember the tune.

"Are they your daughters? They're very pretty," the man finally answered, smiling smugly, dangerously. "Yes, you can. Help me, I mean."

6

The news spread around the already agitated neighborhood like wildfire. Abdelazil, the delivery truck driver, had been beaten up the previous afternoon. Some kids had been threatening a couple from out of town, and he'd tried to step in and help. Of course, the couple was dark skinned. The kids had been warning them they weren't safe, making vague allusions to muggings and airing violent Manichaean conspiracy theories. Abdelazil had been convinced that his status as a local protected him. Maybe he was too full of himself; maybe they just wanted an excuse. One of the kids had hit him in the head with an iron bar, and now he was in the hospital on life support. In the present climate, it apparently didn't take much to turn people into savages.

Jota headed to the gym to see Richard, who was in a much darker mood than before, just like everyone else, but in him it was much more unsettling. He had shady contacts; he knew what was really going on. What sounded like pure speculation when it came from other people, he knew to be fact. Richard was never ruffled by anything, so his expression was a terrible sign. But then Jota reflected that it might be for entirely different reasons. Maybe he'd be able to cheer him up, if only for a moment.

"Don't take this the wrong way, but I don't know how happy I am to be seeing so much of you," Richard began in an ironic tone.

"Do you have any reason to be unhappy?"

"Yes, and so do you."

"Why?"

"I don't think I want to help you anymore. After what happened to Raul, Rodrigo has stationed a car outside. He knows that it's always a good place to begin."

Jota lit a cigarette and stepped into the interior courtyard as though he hadn't heard. "I'm thinking of breaking in somewhere tonight. An antiques shop."

"If I go anywhere with you, we'll have company from our friendly neighborhood cops. You might as well just hand yourself in to Rodrigo."

Jota threw the cigarette away. It wasn't even half-smoked. "Shit, so you won't be coming."

"It's for your own good. Are you going on your own?"

"Yes. I'll have to pick up my old tools."

"Is this still about the clock?"

"Yes. What have you heard?"

"Nothing directly. The guys doing this are pretty careful. And meanwhile, people are chasing ghosts. You saw what happened to that delivery guy. But I've asked around, and one of my guys warned me off. Nobody's saying anything, but they say not to ask questions. These are dangerous people. This might be a tougher nut to crack than you think, Jota, and I won't be there to back you up. Why not just let it go? This isn't like you."

"Why?"

"You know as well as I do. You could easily end up like Diego and Raul."

Jota stared hard at his friend, weighing up the warning. Things were becoming clearer. A warning from Richard was different. It meant that there was good reason to be worried. He reassured himself that he was taking the only option open to him. Whatever happened, the fire would have its way. "I don't know, Richard. There's a lot of pieces to this puzzle that don't seem to fit together."

Jota walked down the street frustrated, trying to think how to arrange the break-in without Richard's help. He knew that he couldn't. He thought about trying to intimidate the old man with threats, but given what Adolfo had told him, he knew he wouldn't be able to get anything out of him. He kept smoking cigarette after cigarette until he realized that he wasn't alone. He cursed his dull instincts. He'd been walking along for quite some time before noticing the two, or maybe three, shadows that were following him. Stupid idiot! He remembered his friends' warnings and was sorry that he hadn't planned things better, that he hadn't been faster and smarter.

Swearing that if he got out of this in one piece, he'd drop the whole thing, he went into the first supermarket he came across as casually as he could. He needed to gain time to plan his escape and make sure that he really was being followed. As he walked down the aisles, he considered his options. Could he call someone? Rodrigo or Richard maybe? If these really were professionals, his friends wouldn't get there in time, and even if it did work out, then he'd have the police on his back. No one had come into the supermarket, so he had some time. If they were as good as people said, they wouldn't risk leaving him on his own in a place that offered so many different options. They'd make sure to keep an eye on him or maybe just remind him that they were there in order to scare him. He considered the possibility that he'd made a mistake, but he knew he was right. Or maybe they weren't that good. That meant he had more leeway. He checked that he still had his knife and bought a broom handle, kitchen roll, lighter fluid, and packing tape. He broke the broom handle right in front of the startled cashier, who wondered whether to call the manager. Eventually she decided just to ignore him: *After all, it's his handle now—he can do what he likes with it.* He wrapped the ends in paper, poured the lighter fluid on them, and joined each half together side by side with the tape to make a firm weapon he could hide under his coat. Then he exited just as casually as he'd entered.

When he'd only gone a few steps, he saw that the three shadows were back, and getting closer and closer. He didn't have much time. Deciding to take what initiative he had left, he turned onto a quieter street and ducked into a handy doorway located just around a corner. He'd kept his pace steady so his pursuers wouldn't react and now readied himself as they approached. He decided not to light the torch; he didn't have enough time, so he just hefted his homemade club. He listened but didn't hear anything. The angle of the light made it hard to see an approaching shadow. He listened harder. He needed to know precisely when the first one came by; he couldn't let the chance go to waste. He listened . . . but suddenly one of them passed by before he could react. Shit, he hadn't heard them. Then he leaped out without thinking, landing three steps away from the next one. He took out his club and swung it hard, hitting the man in the face. The blow was accompanied by a crunch and a spatter of blood that hit his face and arms while the man, who was very young, fell silently to the ground. Jota recognized him. The one in front hadn't yet reacted when Jota dropped the club, took out his knife, and went for the third one, an older man who froze when he saw the boy go down. He hadn't made a sound when Jota, who recognized him too, pressed the knife against his throat.

"Freeze!" He turned to the leader, who tried to decide between lunging at Jota or helping the kid on the ground. The boy was starting to move again, albeit pretty groggily. "You: stay where you are, or I'll slit your dad's throat!"

The man was trembling in fear; the knife cut into his skin. "Boy, do what he says. Make sure that your brother is OK. He can make sure he's OK, can't he, Jota? You might have hurt him."

Jota tried hard to make sense of this Kafkaesque muddle. This was the shop owner who'd commissioned the doll from him, along with his two sons, a couple of knuckleheads who were fine at scaring away the local kids but no match for an adult who knew what he was doing. They'd been sent to intimidate Jota, but he couldn't see how they were connected to the clock. Or the supposed professionals who were apparently behind it all.

"Fuck, of course he can. I've just broken your son's nose," Jota said, withdrawing the knife. "Why the hell were you following me?"

The young man helped up his brother, who looked drunk with his red, swollen face and twin trails of blood dripping from his nostrils.

His father stared at his son as he answered. "We weren't following you."

"No, of course not. It's entirely normal behavior for you to tail someone through the city. You were going to attack me in broad daylight. What's got into you?"

"No, I just wanted to talk to you about a job—"

"I don't do business with stalkers."

"We weren't following you."

The kid helping his brother interjected with a squeak. "You owe us money!"

Jota was taken aback. "What?"

"No, that's not true. The kid's overexcited."

"Tell him, Dad! You're a forger!"

Jota started to put two and two together: the kid's stupid anger and his father's reticence fell into place.

"Well, now at least we're getting somewhere. So I owe you money. Remind me how much, because all I remember is that I gave you a discount on the last job I did for you because the customer couldn't pay any more. You'll have to be a little more precise."

The boy was still angry, puffed up with the indignation of someone who knew they were in the right. "The doll was a fake!"

"Well, fucking hell, what a revelation. That was why your dad hired me—to save half what a real one would have cost. Or didn't he tell you?"

"Well, they don't deal with that side of the business . . ."

The boy looked at his father in surprise.

"It seems that the brother-in-law did a chemical test on it. The plastic wasn't old enough."

"Don't be ridiculous. Since when have I used plastic for a piece from the forties? I only work with celluloid. The sleeping eyes were crystal, and the hair was real. They couldn't have found out it wasn't real. I told you exactly how good the forgery was, and that's what you paid for. I told you that to pass an expert examination would cost you a third more, and you didn't want to pay it, you cheap bastard. But I know my work. The analysis would have cost more than what they paid for the doll."

Jota looked hard into the man's eyes until he saw the hesitation in them. He realized what had happened.

"It wasn't that, was it? You didn't listen to me—you're the same greedy old bastard as ever, and you wanted to keep the rest of the deal for yourself. What else did you sell them? Tell me the truth."

"Nothing—we never saw them again until they came back with their complaint—"

Jota punched him in the nose. A bubble of blood bloomed across the man's jaw. He staggered back, and Jota turned around to face the son, who hadn't yet moved. The father tried to stay on his feet, waving to his boy to stop.

"Son, don't move."

He coughed for a while. Jota, satisfied that the boy would stay where he was, turned back to the father. "So?"

"It was clothes. I thought that after they'd accepted the doll, they wouldn't ask any more questions."

"And now they've caught you with your pants down. But it's because you've lost their trust somehow, you idiot. Anyway, they won't be able to prove it. I promise you that."

The son stared at the man in amazement. "But, Dad—"

"We'll talk later. Help me. I'm dizzy."

Jota let the son sit his brother down against the wall and come over to help his father, the disappointment of disillusionment etched all over his face.

"So you've tried to blame your mess on me. You got the wrong scapegoat. You're just as stupid with your suppliers as you are with your customers."

"Dad . . ."

"I'm sorry, Son. It's the way of the world."

Jota, calmer now, lit a cigarette and looked them up and down with contempt.

"That's right—that's how the world is. The wretched will always stay wretched. Learn that lesson, boy. You'll find it of great use."

He left them to nurse their wounds. A coincidence like that only happened once in your life. The next time it wouldn't be so easy to get away. Jota was running out of time. He decided that he had to act right away, forget about the break-in for now, and complete the first stage of his plan.

Laura had no idea about Jota's setbacks or the warning, and she wouldn't find out in time. She made her plans based on what Jota had told her he would do. After making sure that Adolfo had already visited the store, she left at a time that would ensure she wouldn't bump into him and also gave her enough leeway to get back so Jota would never know she'd left.

On the way there, she began to panic. Three days locked up inside were enough to make the outdoors seem strange and unsettling. She moved around fearfully, with extreme care, hiding until the way was clear, feeling like an intruder in an inhospitable land. It was all so weird to her, like a dream, and she didn't like it. After checking that the store was empty of customers and the old man was on his own—maybe thinking about going home—she went inside with a confidence she'd lacked during the journey there. A false confidence borne of a thirst for redress. The anger of a wronged daughter. The old man was startled to see her: he'd clearly been worried about another kind of visitor.

"Young lady! What a surprise. What can I do for you? You shouldn't have come."

Laura didn't speak. She just stared at him with cold rage.

"I'm sorry. This is a bad time. I was planning to close early and go home . . . if there's something I can help you with, you'll have to come back tomorrow."

"I want the truth."

"Are you still stuck on that business with your father? You need to forget about it. No good can come of this."

"I want the truth. I know about your connection with my father. I know you lied to me."

"I did it for your own good so you wouldn't make the same mistakes I did. But I didn't lie to you. Everything I told you was true."

"I know that my father wasn't killed during a botched robbery."

"What does that matter? Nothing you do will bring him back."

"I'm not leaving without the truth."

The old man thought for a moment. With a glance out the front door, he asked Laura to come in farther. "Go down the stairs. I'll lock up and come join you."

She walked down the worn brick steps to a basement that looked like an old coal cellar, with a couple of high windows that no longer let in any light. It was a small space, packed from floor to ceiling with boxes. There wasn't much furniture, just a couple of wardrobes and a wooden screen separating a wooden desk from the rest. She poked around the cellar for a while before the old man came down.

"Sorry, I'm back. You must forgive me for what I said the other day—I beg you—but your father really was a friend of mine. I . . . I didn't want anything to happen to you . . . I'd rather die than let them hurt you."

"You want me to forgive you? For what? How do you know what happened to me?"

"On the day we spoke, I promise you that I was sincere. I told the truth, but since then they've hurt people. You were right: they're not ordinary thieves. The people who killed Diego have killed others, and I think they might kill me, too, but I don't know who they are."

"So how do you know?"

"The clock you mentioned . . . is it this one?"

The man showed her a printout of a digital photograph. Laura recognized the clock and her father's store behind it. She got the feeling that after weeks of conjecture, she was finally getting somewhere.

"Have you got it?" she said.

"No, I'd never seen it before until I saw this photograph. I asked a man who worked for me a long time ago. A man who found things that were difficult to find."

"A scout?"

"Yes, exactly. Your father and I used to work with a pair of scouts who worked together. They sold that clock to your father, but it came from a lot we split up equally. I imagine that the photograph was taken at the time, for the records. One half of the lot was sold to me. He took the clock just by chance. I never saw it. I asked the man about it, and he brought this photo. I found all this out from him. He told me what was going on, that people were being killed, that he's in danger and so am I, but we don't know why. Here, you can keep this. I'll write down the address he always made out his invoices to; I don't know if it's his real one or not. Plus his telephone number. His name is Xavi. If I talk to him, he might sit down with us and share what he knows, but I don't know how much help he'll be."

"Do you know who my father sold the clock to?"

"The current owner? No, only the scouts know that. I've seen the scout Xavi worked with a few times, but I don't remember what he looks like. He worked with Diego, just like I did with Xavi. We didn't mix and match. That was important to them: they respected each other's clients. A man came in recently asking about that clock. He left, but he'll be back. That's why, young lady . . ."

"Don't worry about him. I know him—he's a friend of mine."

Just then, the old man covered her mouth with his hand and turned toward the stairs. "Quiet. Someone's trying to get in. It might just be a rude customer. I'll go see what's going on. I'm sure everything's fine, but do you see that wardrobe? It has a false back for valuable objects. Get inside, just to be on the safe side."

As he climbed the stairs, Laura went over to the closet, disoriented. He looked back one last time and put his finger to his lips before disappearing from sight. Laura climbed into the closet, trembling with fright. She knew that something was wrong. After she closed the door behind her, voices could be heard upstairs. Then came sounds of a struggle and something breaking. Maybe it was the door being forced open. A few more seconds of silence followed. Then she heard the metal lock give, and there was a loud commotion that came to a sudden stop. She heard footsteps and objects falling to the ground as though everything on the shelves was being knocked down. Then she heard moans, maybe from the old man, and possibly someone hitting him. She couldn't tell; real punches didn't make much noise, not like in the movies. She was too far away to know. Soon afterward, she heard a banging on the stairs, and she eventually made out the blond man's voice.

"We can still do a lot of damage."

This was followed by muffled screams.

"Fuck, gag him! The whole neighborhood will hear!"

"Fucking stubborn old man."

"You heard him. We're not going to get anything out of him."

Laura heard more muffled voices, but she couldn't make them out. While the old man was being tortured, someone was having a casual conversation, like they were talking about the weather. Then she heard the blond man's voice again, and her terrifying experience came back to her vividly. All she could think of was that if she was caught, she'd be killed. Of that she had no doubt.

"Finish up—we need to go. We're out of time. Charlie: search everything. I don't want any surprises."

She heard more struggling, banging, and slapping accompanied by groans of pain. As the sounds of violence died down, she heard boxes being tipped to the floor and closet doors opening. When they opened hers, she bit down on her hand to gag herself. Light filtered into the false back. They ransacked the interior of the closet, and a hand ran along the panels, hovering over the false one. Laura saw a shadow pass a few inches from her nose. She bit down even harder, drawing blood. The shadow closed into a fist and rapped its knuckles as she heard someone going through papers. Hollow. It sounded hollow. The knuckles tapping on the wood gave her away like a skin drum. There was a space behind, and it would only be a moment before they realized it. Then, getting control of her trembling, Laura reached out her hand and placed her palm against the wood, where his knuckles were touching the surface, like a lover's game. The sound changed; it became muffled and dull, as though it were coming through a thick wall. The tapping stopped, and the man moved away.

"That's it."

"Let's go."

She heard steps toward the stairs. For several long minutes, Laura didn't move. She just felt the sweat soaking her back, which felt cold against her T-shirt. Eventually, she took a chance and moved the panel. The closet was empty while the basement had been turned upside down. The owner's body lay at the center of the room in a pool of blood. A cloth had been shoved into his mouth, and his hands were tied behind his back.

Jota waited patiently for his accountant to finish with the previous client and met him with a smile that spoke of a long friendship.

"Well, well, well, Jota in the flesh. What an honor for us mere mortals."

"Yeah, well, you know that I'm not fond of paperwork."

"I've looked into what we spoke about the other day. Everything's ready. You just have to sign this pile of papers."

"Without reading them, of course—best not to read them, eh?"

"You know me too well! But seriously, Jota. Do you really want to do this? I mean, it's yours. You can do what you like with it . . . but selling everything, getting rid of it all?"

"All that matters is that no one knows about this except for you. I'm depending on your discretion. You know I mean it, don't you? If anyone else finds out, even your wife, it could be very dangerous for me."

"Especially if I told my wife!" They laughed at the old joke. "I understand. It's almost ready. We need to visit a notary, and there's a couple of other things."

"There might not be much time."

"Then it's true. This is going to be a total closure."

"Yes."

"Jota, it's been a real pleasure knowing you all these years."

They shook hands, pressing firmly as the melancholy of a definitive goodbye settled around them.

When Laura turned the key in the lock, her hand still trembling with shock, she never expected to find Jota sitting on the sofa with a gin and tonic in his hand. Lacking the energy to lie, she just collapsed on top of him and started speaking before he could even ask.

"Th-they killed him. They've killed him . . . they . . . my God, they killed him. I'm so sorry . . . they killed him!"

Jota had to move quickly to keep her steady before she lost it completely. "What are you talking about? Hush! Why did you go out? Why do you insist on playing detective? Are you trying to get yourself killed?"

"I'm sorry. I'm so sorry . . ."

"Where the hell did you go? I've been going crazy! You understand? I thought something had happened to you! Where the fuck did you go?"

"To the antique shop! To the fucking antique shop you were going to visit. I knew that man! But they came and killed him! They killed him like a dog!"

It took Jota a while to put together the pieces of Laura's incoherent story: she was rambling and frightened. But then he realized that the girl had needed to escape or else she was going to explode. Either she'd been very lucky or had made her own luck. She was a survivor, just like her mother. And he knew that whatever people might think, he wasn't. He knew how to handle himself—he could lie and wriggle out of things, but he had died a long time ago, when he'd lost everything at a stroke, and since then all he'd done was get by. She was different. Laura had followed her instincts, plumbed the depths, and kept going. He'd given up.

Later that night, when Laura was able to talk more calmly about her experience, she gave him the photograph with Xavi's address and telephone number.

"I don't know him. I haven't worked with your father for years. I don't think I know anyone he's been hanging out with recently."

"I don't know . . . I'm so sorry. I wanted . . . I was such an idiot."

"I don't think so. You took an unnecessary risk, sure, but he wouldn't have given this name and address to anyone else. If they couldn't get it out of him, we definitely wouldn't have. So I suppose you had the right idea."

"You think the scout will have the answers?"

"I hope so. It's the only lead we have left."

"I found the cat's window. You hid it behind an old bookcase."

"I'll have to block it up one day."

"But you leave food out for him."

"I can't let him starve!"

Laura smiled, fascinated by this strange, inconsistent man. She began to feel safe again. As her mind relaxed, she noticed that something about the photograph of the clock was wrong, but she didn't know what.

Jota studied the address closely. After making sure that he was at the right place, he went to the buzzer and rang it, keeping his finger pressed down for a long time. He stood waiting, smiling at a woman coming out of the building. He rang again without getting an answer. He had intentionally come to the building at the most unlikely time for someone to be home, when most people were at work. A few minutes later, another resident came in and held the door open.

"Would you like to come in?"

"No, thank you. I'm waiting for someone to come down."

The man went inside and let the door swing shut behind him. Jota slipped a folded metro ticket into the lock, waited for the resident to disappear, and went in. He took the elevator, came out onto the landing, and looked around. He rang the doorbell twice, listened discreetly at the door, and once he was sure it was safe, stuck small pieces of tape over the peepholes on the doors of the neighboring apartments and then started to pick the lock. After examining it for a moment, he took an X-ray sheet from his coat and slipped it into the gap. The door opened easily, and he held it open so it wouldn't make a sound. Before going inside, he removed the tape from the doors, and then he slipped in silently. He listened to make sure that it was empty and closed the door gently. His mind was alive with thoughts long since buried; it was as though he was remembering his training. He didn't know if it was a house or an office or even if this Xavi lived alone. He very carefully checked each room one by one. Fine, there was no one in the apartment, but whoever did live there hadn't bolted the door, so they probably hadn't gone far. Jota assumed that he didn't have much time.

He quickly moved around the apartment, which was full of well-organized, cataloged antiques set out across different rooms in boxes and display cases. This Xavi was a stickler for tidiness and order. Jota was a little jealous; suddenly he felt a bout of malice toward him. "Bastard," he muttered to himself. He went over to a desk containing several carefully arranged folders and opened a card holder in which he found Diego's card. Next to it was a leather journal with lots of notes and a long list of telephone numbers. He picked it up. Next he found cabinets full of folders organized by year and took the most recent ones. They were full of photographs, dates, and explicatory notes.

Xavi was young, handsome, and elegantly dressed. He'd found his way into the weird world of collectors through interior design. The path had been a strange one. He came from a wealthy family and had plenty of charm; women had always been easy to come by, but he'd been drawn to the shady subculture of antiques, the thrill of stealing, of living life to the fullest, getting your hands dirty searching for a piece in a gloomy underworld populated by losers. It was a marked contrast to the life he'd known. Xavi didn't make a living from it; he was just slumming. If a job excited him, he took it; if not, he walked away. Because he could.

Xavi opened the door to his building, completely oblivious to what was going on in his home—and to the fact that at that very moment, the body of one of his regular customers was being put in a body bag. The owner of the antiques store had spent the night in the basement until his baker neighbor had noticed that his door had been left ajar and gone in to find out what had happened. Xavi opened the door to the building and, out of habit, checked his mailbox as he waited for the elevator.

Jota put the folders he'd gathered in a bag and went to the door, pleased with what he'd found and the fact that it had gone so smoothly. He locked up carefully and went to the elevator, which was already on its way up. Instinctively, because he hadn't pressed the button, he headed for the stairs as a precaution. He'd barely gone a couple of steps when he heard the elevator arrive and open. Knowing that this could be dangerous, he sped up and started to take the stairs two by two.

Xavi came out of the elevator and heard the sound of rapid footsteps but didn't see anyone. He headed for his door. It only took a glance for him to see marks on the lock and frame that anyone else would have missed, and he chided himself for being so lax. He dropped the grocery bags and ran down the stairs, knowing that he was quicker than the elevator.

Jota wasn't in such great physical shape. He heard the footsteps approaching behind him before he got to the ground floor. He was tempted to slow down and let them catch up. Maybe the person in the elevator hadn't been heading for the apartment, or maybe they hadn't even noticed he was there. He'd been very discreet. But the footsteps echoed behind him, and he looked up to see Xavi only a couple of flights above him. Shit! He went as fast as he could, but it was obvious that the younger, faster man might catch him. He got to the door but couldn't see how it opened. He tried to find the button—where was it? He was running out of time. Suddenly a woman appeared, heading out. Maybe Lady Luck was smiling on him after all. He leaped for the door and pushed the woman aside. She dropped a trash bag onto the floor while he let one of the folders slip. He knew that he didn't have time to pick it up. With the woman's imprecations ringing in his ears, he crossed the street without looking, simply trusting to dumb luck that there wouldn't be any cars coming his way, and disappeared around the corner. Xavi was met by the swearing woman and slipped on a puddle of orange liquid. He had to stop running to stay upright and knew that he'd lost a crucial few seconds. He headed outside and looked around frantically but soon gave up. The empty street glared back at him. Then he calmly turned around, picked up the folder, and went back inside to help the woman.

Jota slipped into his car. He was walking on air, high on a rush of excitement he hadn't felt in years. He felt alive. Life was suddenly worth the effort, and even dealing with the shit the city had to throw at him seemed worth it. A fog of uncertainty spread out before him. He was on the trail of his prey, the scent was in his nostrils, and he was jubilant at the prospect of undoing the damage of the past. Jota felt both alive and also, briefly, as though he were living in another time. For a moment he thought he could control the fire again or even put it out. Maybe he'd be able to close another wound.

Adolfo heard the car parking outside. A new Jota bounced in through the door. He was rejuvenated, barely recognizable; there was a novel but also familiar gleam in his eyes. The old Jota was back. Rather late, but back all the same. Jota came in and dropped several folders on his desk.

But Adolfo didn't react. He didn't want to see Jota. He didn't want anything to do with this. Maybe Jota thought he might win the battle, but he'd already lost. All Adolfo could think of was his terrified wife, the threats the killers had made, and his two innocent girls. This business could not darken their door again. They had the right to be happy and never come into contact with his shitty life. His two girls were in danger. That was all that mattered.

"What are you doing here?"

"Look!" Jota jubilantly opened one of the accordion folders and took out a plastic file with several old photographs inside. "It's all the fucking pieces in the collection. This is our guy: he's as diligent as a monk, the finicky bastard."

His partner looked though them in fear and frustration. "There aren't many here. It's missing half at least . . . the precious clock is missing."

"I have that already. If the information I have is accurate, he didn't sell the clock, but I don't care. It's him. He sold the rest along with another scout. Now we have to get him to give us the name. I'm just a step away—get it? One step. We need to . . . I have to talk to Richard . . . we have to. I still don't know how . . ."

As Jota excitedly chattered away, Adolfo's suspicions were confirmed. A youthful flame had been reignited in Jota. He looked like one of those people ready to take on the world. Older and sadder than he had been, maybe, but this was the real Jota, back from the dead.

Jota lit a cigarette that he finished in three puffs as he proudly held up his trophy. His partner didn't dare complain about the smoke. The more excited Jota got, the more Adolfo felt the fear building. The fuse had been lit, and he knew that there was nothing that could stop it now. This only led one way for him and his children.

"Richard? Have you gone crazy? What are you planning to do? You have to stop it! You're going to get yourself killed, just like Diego. And me along with you!"

Jota looked up in surprise. "What's wrong? Don't you see? We're winning. This time we're going to fucking win!"

"Are you still playing your game? Can't you see that it's not real?"

Just then Jota's phone started to ring. He didn't recognize the number. "Hello?"

"Hello, Jota."

"Who is this?"

"It's Xavi. I think we met briefly, or at least I'm familiar with the back of you. I became acquainted with it as you left my building this morning. You're pretty quick for a man of your age."

Jota thought hard about what to say next. "How did you find me? You might be in serious trouble, young man. I only want names. If you give them to me, then you'll be out of it."

"The buyer's name? You won't find that in my files. I don't know if you know what's at stake here, for both of us. But compared to what we're up against, you *and* me, any threats you make are small beer."

"Are you sure?"

"You're on the list now too."

"Who's your partner?"

Xavi giggled before saying, "This isn't the right time to tell you that. But we can all help each other out. He gave me your telephone number. I'm going to leave town tomorrow, but I have information you might find useful. If what I've heard is true, there might still be something you can do."

"Why would you give it to me?"

"Because they're going to kill me. That's good enough reason, don't you think? And if I give it to you, maybe you'll have a chance to work things out. Or maybe they'll kill you. If you work things out, I can go into hiding for a while and come back once things have calmed down, or . . . well, I win either way."

"Give it to me."

"No, not over the phone. You know where I live. Obviously I'm not there. If you found it, they might have too. I'll be going by to pick up my things tomorrow. I leave for the station at eight in the morning. Let's meet at the café opposite, at seven. All three of us. I'll tell you everything there. Then I'll disappear. I have some answers, but they won't help me. They might you."

"What if I don't come?"

"Then I'll have to disappear forever, I'm afraid. And what good will that do you? I'll have a suitcase with me. Oh, please bring me back my journal and card holder—they won't be of any use to you, and I need them. The journal isn't even real leather."

And with that, Xavi hung up. Jota called back again and again, but a mechanical voice told him that the phone had been switched off. When he finally gave up, Adolfo handed him the journal and the folders.

"Here, take these. I'm going home to be with my daughters. I want nothing more to do with this."

"What?"

"I mean it. You have no right . . . I'm not chasing around after you anymore. No . . . just go."

"What the hell is wrong with you?"

"I have a family, get it? No . . . I can't do this anymore."

"But this is almost over."

"Exactly! It's too late to fix what happened twenty years ago! Don't you see? This is different—this is a different girl! Your best friend died, and you'll never be able to fix that. What good do you think finding out who killed Diego is going to do? That only makes sense in your head! It was all over a long time ago. This has nothing to do with it!"

Jota didn't answer. There was nothing he could say. Adolfo walked Jota outside in silence, locked the door behind him, and walked off without looking back.

The cat was sitting in Laura's lap, purring. She looked at the photograph of the clock again and again. Her father's home, the shop floor. It all looked right, and yet something didn't fit. Something was irritating her. Laura stared and stared at the dirty wall, the desk in the background, the table lamp. It was all there, and yet it was wrong. She stared at it for so long that when she closed her eyes, the negative image appeared behind her eyelids. But she couldn't solve the puzzle.

Suddenly, the cat turned toward the door, but instead of hissing as usual, he arched his back. His hair stood on end while his tail went puffy and rigid. Then he growled harshly and ran away from the door, toward the window. Laura jumped up, aware that something was wrong. She carefully approached the front door and listened. Then she heard whispers and scratching and realized that someone was trying to break in.

She quickly picked up her shoes, bag, and the folder and ran out toward the cat's window. She moved the bookcase just enough for her to get by, then pulled it back again to cover her tracks. Then she quietly crawled outside, scratching and dirtying herself, and headed into the darkness. Before her stretched the dark roofs of the old city. Surveying the scene, she knew where she had to go.

"Remember: any trace, any clue. We just need the girl. We don't have much time, and he's good. He can't know we were here."

They spread out around the house, oblivious to the hidden window. They soon found her clothes.

"Hey . . . take a look at this."

"What? What's this?"

"The bed, the socks, the food . . ."

"Shit! Fucking hell! She was here the whole time. She's fucking been here the whole time!"

"But he was looking for her—"

"Because he's smarter than you are! He knew we'd hear about it. He's a smart son of a bitch."

"But she's not here."

"He must have moved her without our noticing. Shit. Is anyone on him right now?"

"No, we're here and on Xavi."

"Shit, shit, shit. He's one step ahead of us. Fine, nothing changes. Let's go; there's nothing we can do here."

"I don't know. There's something strange about all this."

"What?"

"The clothes, the food . . . it's like she was still here."

"Are we sure she isn't hiding? Search every last inch of this place."

"But then he'll know we were here."

"If we want him to lead us to her, maybe he should know. Turn this place upside down—quick. We can't be too long. Where might he have taken her?"

"A hostel maybe. She could be anywhere."

"Shit, shit, shit. We had her! She was right in our grasp. What do you think, Richard?"

Richard walked away from his men to speak to the blond man. "Don't worry; we're almost there. We have them all, don't we? That's why you hired me. It's just a question of being patient. It's Jota's weakness. Only Xavi and the other scout are left. We need to calm down. Jota will lead us to them, and when we've finished them off, he'll lead us straight to the girl—he'll have no choice. And that's if he doesn't come to ask me for help first. We just have to follow him. Xavi and the girl are as good as dead."

7

Jota parked the car with a bittersweet feeling. His success with Xavi had been undermined by his frustration with Adolfo and the fear he'd seen in his friend's eyes. What had changed? Maybe Adolfo was right about him chasing ghosts from twenty years ago. But then he thought about Laura, a girl who'd lost her father. She was so similar to her mother. She'd been little more than a girl back then. And he'd been just a boy. They'd all been children.

Jota knew what he was going to do. Maybe he shouldn't, but he was going to do it anyway. The fire was burning away inside him, and only one thing would extinguish it now. It had lodged in his soul, intense and destructive. The fire now defined his entire existence and would keep raging until he'd seen this through to the end, even if that meant the end of him too. He knew what might happen and how easily it might all go wrong. He knew what was at stake, just as Xavi had reminded him. They might all end up dead: Xavi, him, maybe Adolfo. But Laura couldn't end up like that—she was too young. She'd lost too much in too short a time. She'd given too much already. Hope, a reason to live, the fire gave him everything. Before he went home, Jota went to see his accountant to finish up the paperwork he'd been preparing for several days.

When he got home, late, something in the air felt wrong. His front door was open. The lock had been forced, and he saw immediately that it had been left that way to send a message. They wanted him to know that they'd been there. Just in case, he took out his knife and slowly pushed the door open. He felt his way in the dark and looked around: everything was a mess. Knowing it was pointless, he began to search, whispering into the darkness. He was acting instinctively, the way you did at stressful times. Hoping against hope.

"Laura?"

He went through each room in turn, getting increasingly desperate.

"Laura? Fuck!"

Almost certain of the worst, he felt for his phone. There was still hope, he told himself. If they'd killed her, the body would still be there. They wouldn't have bothered to take it anywhere. Maybe they'd want to make a deal. If they had taken her, she must still be OK—at least she was alive. His hands shaking, he dialed her number, expecting to hear a man's voice issuing instructions or making demands. But there she was, whispering, relaxed: she was safe, unharmed.

"Jota, are you at home? I'm fine. Nothing's happened to me. Someone was trying to break in, but I got out through the window. They didn't see me. I wasn't followed."

"Laura! Laura! My God! Are you OK? Did they do anything to you? Has anything happened? Tell me the truth. Are you alone? Are you safe?"

"You aren't listening to me. I'm fine—safe and sound. No one knows where I am. Don't worry."

"Forgive me—it was my fault. I left you alone for too long. I was just asking for them to find you. I was overconfident. Forgive me. Where are you? I'll come pick you up. From now on you stick with me."

"No, Jota. I think that now I'm safer on my own. Also . . . I think . . . I'm not sure yet, but I think I might have something. I know it's somewhere in my brain. I just can't access it."

"Laura, I'm going to pick you up, wherever you are. I won't leave you—"

"Jota, just listen, please. They found your house. They might know that I was there. Well, they definitely will if they're not complete idiots." She laughed caustically. "What if they're watching you? I'm not sure that I'm safe with you. I think I almost have it, just . . . leave me alone tonight. You can pick me up tomorrow and take me to your friend Rodrigo, OK? Please, please. Just tonight. I'll be safer that way."

"This isn't a negotiation, I can't leave you alone. What if they find you?"

"They already would have."

"No, Laura, this is the last word. Where are you?"

"Then you leave me no choice." Laura hung up on him.

Knowing that she wouldn't answer anymore, Jota threw the phone against the wall. He kicked the detritus of his ruined apartment across the floor until he finally got control of himself. Surprisingly, the phone was still working. He couldn't stay where he was. He found a chain to lock the door and left the mess behind.

He spent the rest of the night driving around, smoking cigarette after cigarette, struggling with his anxiety, trying to kill the hours left until dawn, when he'd be able to tie up the loose ends and find the person responsible before Laura got hurt. His eyes burned with the intensity of the flame; his scar throbbed. His battle with time grew more excruciating with every minute. All he could do was wait, drive, and wait some more. When it was almost two in the morning, he stopped in front of Diego's shop and kept watch for a while. He knew she was there. The stupidest place in the world, where no one would think to look for her. She was in there. He got as far as reaching for the doorknob but then thought twice. He looked into his rearview mirror and checked the street suspiciously. The night was bathed in an orange glow. No one was there. He thought again, started the car, and drove on.

After speaking to Jota on the phone, Laura sat in the position the camera had been when the photo of the clock had been taken. She looked at the space again and again, until she'd memorized every detail, comparing them to those in the image. Everything was there. There was no doubt about it. It was exactly the same, and yet it still didn't fit. Then she thought about the invoices. The paperwork was from five years ago, when the transaction had been done. Her head lit up with an idea.

Jota was dozing in his seat when a passing ambulance woke him up. He'd slept in an awkward position, and now his neck hurt. He checked the time: 5:30 a.m. He got out of the car. He went into an open café and ordered a cognac. Time seemed to have stopped moving. He asked for change for the cigarette machine. Then he checked his watch again: 6:30 a.m. He paid the bill and left the café. He walked down a street, still checking the time. Now it was 6:50 a.m. He could see Xavi's building in the distance. Then he saw a pair of ambulances, and he slowed down before running forward again.

People had gathered around a police cordon. Several officers were blocking their way, hiding a body covered in a metallic gold blanket. Jota spoke to the man next to him.

"What happened?"

"A tragedy, a real tragedy."

Another man chimed in. "The kid killed himself."

Soon a woman came over with tears in her eyes. "I saw it. It was horrible. It was awfu . . ." she broke down into a melodramatic bout of sobbing and couldn't go on.

The first man consoled her disinterestedly. "There, there, it's over now."

Jota moved on and turned to a woman speaking to a policeman. "Do you know what happened?"

The policeman answered. "Are you a relative of the victim?"

"No, I've come to meet someone. But I can't find them."

Then the woman answered. "It was the boy in 6B."

Jota knew the apartment: he'd been in there just a day before. It was Xavi, no doubt about it.

The policeman noticed his reaction and grew curious. "Did you know him?"

"No."

"Then please move on; there are too many people around here already."

The woman spoke between sobs. "I was just talking to him only a little while ago."

The policeman turned to her. "Really, what did he say?"

"Oh, he was such a nice boy . . . he said he was going up to get a suitcase. He was going on a trip . . ."

"Amazing. A suitcase. Some trip he went on."

"He was so polite—who would have thought it?"

"The best always die young. And we're all that's left," the policeman summed up with all the gravity of a heartfelt platitude. He and the woman began to exchange a series of truisms and clichés.

"Did he say where he was planning on going?" Jota interrupted.

"Oh, don't be morbid," the policeman exclaimed in indignation.

"I asked, but he just laughed and said the bus station."

"The bus station."

"Yes, he said that no one would think to look for him there. Buses! Oh, my boy! Oh my God! If I'd have known what he was really talking about . . ."

The policeman led her back to familiar territory. "Oh, you never know. One moment you're here, and the next . . ."

Jota walked off into the crowd, stumbling toward his car like a sleepwalker or a ghost. He hadn't slept much, but this felt like a waking nightmare. Jota got into his car and sat for half an hour with no idea what to do. They'd gotten to Xavi first. What could he do now? He'd hit a dead end. Only the other scout was left, and after this he'd never be able to find him. He went over their conversation again and again. When someone gave you all the information, you didn't bother scrutinizing it. "He gave me your phone number." Jota opened the journal and started to read the names one by one. "He gave me your phone number." What if he knew him? What if he knew the other scout? Maybe someone in the diary could help him. Or at least set him on the right track. But none of the pages gave him what he was looking for. "He gave me your phone number." Then he got to *S*. A surname. Rafa's surname. It had been him all along, shit. Rafa. He'd never stopped working for Diego. Just another lie from a pair of huge liars who liked to keep their business secret. Speculation, no more than that. But no, it was Rafa. Who else could it be? Did Xavi say that he was getting out of there? He was, but was Rafa too? Could he just leave like that, disappear? They'd planned to meet, but Rafa had obligations, businesses. Then again, he could well be that desperate. Jota knew that he was minutes, maybe hours, behind. He didn't have a second to lose.

The neighborhood was tense; the atmosphere was claustrophobic. There were more and more incidents—a demonstration had been planned for that afternoon to protest the high crime rate. People's opinions were quickly getting polarized. Jota was going as quick as he could. He was desperate. People had stopped talking in the street; they just looked around fearfully. He went into a café. The people having breakfast at the bar turned around, and one or two said hello.

The barman looked up as he served coffee. "What's up, big man? What can I do for you?"

"Is Rafa here?"

"Not today. I was just saying how strange it was. He's usually here by now."

"Do you know where he might be?"

"Well, it's Thursday today, isn't it? He's probably at the customs office, dealing with the new shipments."

The barman served another coffee. When he looked back up, Jota had left.

Jota was driving like a man possessed, burning up with flames that would never go out, the flames that drove him on and threatened to destroy him. Every second counted. He got to the industrial estate by the airport and parked by the guard post outside the customs building. Several tired-looking people were waiting in a room next to a vacant window. Movement could be heard on the other side. Eventually, a little man appeared and came to the window, but none of the people waiting went over to him. He called to Jota.

"You: have you come to pick up something?"

"No, I'm looking for a customs agent, Rafael Sanz."

"Rafael?"

"He comes on Thursdays. He must have arrived a little while ago."

"Oh yeah, I know him. He hasn't come in yet, but he won't be long; he has boxes to pick up. You can wait over there."

Jota sighed, sat down, and took out a cigarette.

"You can't smoke in here."

Jota sighed harder and went outside.

Carlos, Laura's uncle, walked into his dead brother's shop and got the fright of his life. She was sitting waiting for him, surrounded by piles of paperwork.

"Laura! Damn it. What are you doing here? What's wrong?"

She smiled darkly at him.

"What?"

"Hello, Uncle. I've been doing some paperwork, but I haven't had time to tidy up yet."

"Are you all right? What's going on?"

"Oh, nothing. How are you?"

"I don't understand. What's that on your face? You're not well. I'm calling your mother."

Laura pointed to the original receipt for the clock and said, "Is this a sales receipt?"

"Stay there—I'm calling your mother."

"Tell me! Is this a sales receipt?"

Her uncle froze. He'd never seen his niece act like this. "I don't know. I suppose so."

"Yes, you do! You noted it down here! Sold!"

"Yes, you're right. I wrote it down."

"What does it mean?"

"Nothing. I'm going through the whole archive—it's huge. You know how your father worked."

"No, I don't. I never worked with him. But you did, for years."

"Well, I've been trying to inventory all the remaining stock."

"Did he sell this clock five years ago?"

"How should I know?"

"Look at this: it's the clock in his office."

"Yes, it is. So? He must have taken the photo for a sale or for his inventory."

"Five years ago?"

"I guess."

"That's what's thrown me all this time. I've been staring at this photo for two days, and I couldn't work out why. But you know what? Now I have. Because of the lamp behind it. That shitty little lamp. My dad showed it to me less than a year ago because he was proud of his find. I didn't give a shit. I'd forgotten all about it, but now I know. This photo wasn't taken five years ago. It was taken a month ago. The clock was always here, and now you've sold it. God knows to whom."

"Your father stored a few things in a warehouse—he kept some of the stock there because it was safer or something. It was a secret he kept with someone he knew. No one knew he used it, not even the owner of the warehouse. I knew about it from when we worked together."

"And when he moved things there, he issued a receipt."

"Of course, to keep track. That's why there wasn't a sales price. He just wrote *W* for *warehouse*."

"He never sold the clock."

"No, it was in the warehouse."

"There never was a buyer. No one was worried about being found—we've been chasing a mirage this whole time. He just wanted to sell it. And now you and your buddy have sold it like it was any old piece."

"Yes, of course. I don't know what . . ."

"You sold the clock even though you knew that it was why your brother had been killed!"

"I don't know what you mean."

"Yes, you do! You know everyone! You know very well! You just wanted to get rid of everything so you could look the other way!"

"That's not true."

"He was your brother, but more importantly he was my dad. I want the address of the warehouse."

Jota finished a cigarette in his car and dropped the butt next to the other five. He checked his watch again, annoyed to be wasting time. He had no idea if Rafa would come or not. But he had to—he couldn't leave merchandise in customs, or it might get returned. Was he scared enough to cut out on a deal? That didn't seem likely, not even in these circumstances. Maybe there was another option Jota hadn't taken into account. By way of an answer, a figure appeared. Jota's eyes burned: Gabriel, Rafa's assistant, his face still bruised from the beating Jota had given him. Jota got out of his car and stood in his way. When Gabriel saw him, he tried to turn and run, but he still couldn't move very fast. Jota jumped on his back, and they both fell to the ground. Then he turned Gabriel over and hit him twice in the face, and then he covered Gabriel's mouth and started to bark orders.

"Tell me where Rafael is. I won't ask twice."

Gabriel sized up his threatening visage and nodded. Jota took his hand away.

"He called me this morning to tell me to pick up an order. I saw him for a second to get the paperwork—here, I have it with me."

"Why? Where did he go?"

"I thought you knew. He said he had a meeting with you and Xavi, and then they'd be taking a bus, leaving their cars behind. He was going to contact me in a few days. Then this morning he called to say that there'd been a change of plans. He couldn't come to pick up the order today, so I had to come instead. That's all he told me."

"Xavi's dead. He was killed a few hours ago. Where was Rafa going—when did he leave?"

"I don't know. I don't know anything about this. He said he'd be taking a bus because it was a good way to get away incognito, but I don't know when or where he was going. I only saw him an hour ago. He probably hasn't left yet."

Jota hid Gabriel's car at one end of the lot. Then he bound and gagged Gabriel in his seat. Gabriel meekly allowed himself to be tied up, offering no resistance. Jota took his phone.

"Don't try to escape. I'll be back for you."

Jota's car roared off toward the bus station. The ticket counter was sixty feet long and milling with travelers of all kinds. Jota went to look at the departures board to check the different destinations. Then he walked around the entire station, peering at faces and bodies. He went down to the platforms and searched the buses through the windows. Then he went back up and walked through the stores and restaurant. It was very possible that he'd missed him. He did a second tour of the ticket offices and crowds. Then he went back to the shopping area. Suddenly, he saw Rafa in a candy store, carrying a suitcase. Jota waited patiently for him to come out and came up behind him. He put an arm around him, the point of his knife discreetly pressed against Rafa's flesh.

"Hello, Rafa. I know you weren't expecting me, but here I am. Let's have a little chat before you leave. I have absolutely no problem cutting a chunk into your back. It wouldn't be fatal, but I doubt you'll be hard to find in hospital."

Rafa didn't answer. They walked together down a narrow corridor, past a cleaning cart. Then they went down to a platform and slipped into an empty bathroom. Jota locked the door from the inside. He knocked Rafa down and then lifted him up again. Rafa looked at him in surprise.

"Are you with them? Are you going to kill me?"

"Who are they?"

"How should I know?"

"Then what do you know? What was Xavi going to tell me? Were you going to meet him at seven?"

"No. He was going to meet you alone. We didn't know what you were planning. If you came to an agreement, he was going to call me to come meet up. If I didn't get a call from him, we'd each go our separate ways. We wouldn't know where the other was going. But he was sure you'd play ball, so I was surprised when he didn't call. I ignored what we'd said and called him. When he didn't answer, I went to his apartment. I saw what happened."

"And you decided to run away."

"I wasn't planning on going. I thought we were safe. Xavi was the one who wanted to leave by bus—it was the easiest way to escape without anyone knowing. I went along with him because I didn't think it'd be necessary. When I got to his apartment, I realized that I really did have to disappear. I thought you were dead too."

"You gave him my phone number."

"Of course. When you broke into his apartment, he thought that they'd found him, but when he gave me a description, I knew it was you. He thought you were his last chance. He knew that after the old man, he was the only one left."

"So why were you safe?"

"Because otherwise I'd have been killed the day after Diego. You've come because of that, haven't you? To find out why."

"Yes."

"It all began with the clock you were looking for, our clock, the one Diego sold."

"How did you know about it?"

"Because I got it for him five years ago. No one ever mentioned it again. Then you came along like a bull in a china shop, ransacking all the different suppliers for a worthless clock."

"How did he find out that I was looking for it?"

"I found out. It was your clock man. He had the photo on his workbench. I went to pick up a job and saw it. I recognized it immediately. You know the old man—he tried to play dumb, but I got him to spill his guts in about ten minutes. You never knew who to trust. I didn't like what I heard, so I went to talk to Diego. He didn't care about the clock; he just wanted to screw you. He said that he could get it without any trouble and offered to cut me in if I could track down your client. I told him that I wasn't interested."

"Yeah, you were too honest. Don't give me that shit."

"You can believe whatever you like, but I never heard anything more about it. I didn't want anything to do with it. You think if I'd been involved, Diego would have had to send Raul to get his information? Diego didn't know how to do that kind of thing. I charged a commission for the information and forgot all about it."

"Why?"

"Because I had the clock once, and I don't ever want to see it again."

"Where did you get it?"

"From a house in the country."

"The kind you used to burgle."

"I didn't burgle; I did deals."

"Yeah, like you always do."

"Don't get the wrong idea. I haven't done that kind of thing for a long time."

"Go on."

"It was an easy job. The information came from a security guard: the house didn't have any security systems, and there was plenty of money inside. It was going to be empty that weekend. I called Xavi, but our usual guys weren't available that weekend. He found other people, two professionals. But the information turned out to be shit, and everything went wrong. There wasn't anything of value in the house, and it wasn't empty. The owners were still there, an old couple. While we were going through the living room, the other two guys went up to the bedrooms and found them. They weren't professionals—they were a pair of fucked-up drug addicts looking for trouble. We heard what they were doing. By the time we got there, they'd killed them. We ran the hell out of there and never saw them again."

"Yeah, yeah, stop. You're bringing tears to my eyes."

"It wasn't normal. You should have seen . . . they were sick. I never did another break-in. I don't know if Xavi did, but I didn't. The lot was worthless. It was so easy to trace."

"And this wasn't just a robbery."

"Right, it was a double murder. We split the lot as usual: Xavi got one half, and I got the other. He sold his to the old man, and I sold mine to Diego. He never cared where the lots came from. I got the clock. It was just a coincidence. Diego decided to store it away until it was safe. I didn't see it again until the photograph at your clock man's shop. It was a shock. It reminded me of a horrible experience."

"So you tell Diego, and he decides to go get the clock. And they get him."

"Yeah. Right from the start, I knew there was a connection, but I didn't want to get involved."

"Is there any chance it was worth more than you thought?"

"Huh, like a hidden jewel? You tell me. You're the one looking for it."

"I'm not anymore."

"Oh, I'm so pleased," Rafa said sarcastically. "Let's tell Xavi. It'll be a big help to him. This isn't about what the clock is worth—forget it. There's no hidden secrets. I've seen it. I've held it in my hands. At first I thought that Diego had a problem with the current owner, but for some other reason, not the clock. Maybe something related to where it came from . . . or Raul . . . maybe he tried to steal it or something, but that couldn't be right either. If it had been worth something or had some connection to where it is now, I would have followed right after Diego."

"If they knew where it came from . . ."

"Of course, so as the days went by, I knew I was safe. No one was looking for me, and I didn't give them any reason to. But then they got the old man. It made no sense: the old man didn't have anything to do with the clock. Why kill him and not me? Xavi thought he was in danger, and so did I. If they weren't following me, he had nothing to fear either. Obviously, I was wrong."

"Maybe it was the other robbers?"

"Why? Plus, they didn't know Diego or the old man. They'd have killed us first. You're not seeing it, Jota, just like I didn't want to admit it until this morning. Xavi was very smart. He did see it: they got them, our 'partners,' first. They're both dead: one a while ago as he was trying to steal a car. The other just a couple of months ago. They slit his throat in the middle of the street. They'd killed them before you started looking for anything. I didn't want to believe it, but Xavi was right. There was a list. It was just a list, and we were last on it."

"So you don't think it has anything to do with the clock? What else did Xavi know that might help me? Why did he think that I'd be able to help you?"

"I don't know, but it doesn't matter now. You found me, and they will too. Open your eyes: nobody else is left. They'll kill me and maybe you next. There's no one else, Jota. No one."

"You're wrong. There is somebody. I need to undo a path I should have undone a while ago instead of heading blindly forward like an idiot. You could come back with me and try to get to the bottom of this."

"Thank you, Jota, but I want to take my last chance. They might well be here already. They've probably found us."

Jota took note of these words as he came out of the bathroom. He went out of the station, scanning his surroundings. Had they found him? Could they have followed him from Xavi's apartment? He couldn't see the blond man watching from an upper floor, letting him go while he stayed near the bathroom where Rafa had been left sitting on the floor, staring straight ahead.

Laura, covered in sweat and dust, walked past several warehouses. She went over to a man in work overalls.

"Excuse me, can you tell me where the Torres antiques warehouse is?"

"Over there, on Yunque Street. It's the third one. The shop is the first, and the biggest one is the warehouse."

Fran, Torres's foreman, was cleaning his face after going through the most recent delivery of merchandise. A worker came over.

"Boss, there's a girl looking for you."

He turned around in surprise and recognized Laura immediately. "Hello, you're Diego's daughter. Who are you looking for?"

"You. You're Fran, aren't you? My uncle told me about you. I've come for something that belongs to me."

"Listen, I know you're going through a hard time—"

"I'm seeing this through to the end. Anything you don't give me now, I'll report to the police as stolen."

"If you've come to threaten me, there's the door."

"Fine. I'll be back." She turned around and walked off decisively without looking back.

He watched her go but called out before she got to the door. "Wait! How do you know I have what you're looking for?"

Laura took out a photo of the clock. "You lied to Jota, didn't you? I know that too."

"Come with me."

He led her into the back, where there was a hallway lined by small rooms. "Your father did business with me for years. He kept things here that he needed hidden for a while, for various different reasons. It was a deal we had; no one else knew about it."

"Stolen things?"

"Not just that. They call them 'stained.' They're problematic pieces. A few weeks ago he came to get back a piece he'd had in the warehouse for years."

"The clock."

As they spoke, they went into one of the rooms. Fran unlocked a chain, went in alone, and came back out with a box.

"Here."

It was the clock, the one from Jota's photograph, the one from Raul's photograph. A chunk of metal that had led to the deaths of who knew how many people. Her father had had it all this time, with it only ever leaving the warehouse for a stupid photo.

"Why did he bring it back?"

"Because he wanted to keep it here, I suppose. I don't ask questions."

"Is it worth much?"

"No. Take it."

Laura held the clock in her hands and waited for the sign-off.

"Do you know why I'm giving it to you?"

"So I won't report you."

"Give me the photograph."

She handed it to him, and he tore it up, putting the pieces in his pocket.

"Report what you like. I've helped you. I expect the same of you. You were never here; we never met. Say what you like about the clock, that your father kept it in the basement maybe, but never tell Jota about this. He must never know that I hid it from him. That's my only condition."

Laura just nodded.

"So I have your word. Now go."

Laura was sitting at a suburban bus stop looking at the clock. She took a card out of her pocket and made a call.

Clara Morgades was looking through some bills when her internal line buzzed.

"Yes?"

"Diego Blanco's daughter on the phone."

The name was a shock. It took her a few moments to react. "Did you say Diego Blanco?"

"Yes, she says she's his daughter, Laura. I don't know her."

"Put her through."

Laura heard the call get passed on.

"Hello?"

"Is this Clara Morgades?"

"Yes."

"I'm Diego's daughter. I have the clock."

"I think you must be mistaken."

"Jota was only forging a new one. I have the real one, and I want to know what it's worth."

"I'm not looking for a clock. That commission was canceled."

"I have a note about your meeting with my father. Given how his friends tend to act, I imagine you're still interested. I want to know how much you're willing to pay for it."

"Can you prove to me that you have it?"

"We could meet."

"No tricks now. That's very important."

"Not on either side."

At the bus station, the cleaning lady walked slowly along the service hall, dragging her cart behind her in desultory fashion. She headed for the men's bathroom.

"Hello? Is anyone in here? Cleaning!"

When she got no answer, she put out her yellow sign, went inside, and started to open the doors to the stalls. One of the doors wouldn't open; something was blocking it. She pushed harder but could barely move it any farther. Then she realized that the floor was slippery. She had stepped into a pool of red liquid that had oozed out from beneath the door. On the other side, Rafa's lifeless body was slumped against the door, blood still flowing from his neck.

The afternoon was coming to an end. The blond man gravely observed the commotion in the hall opposite. People were gathering, shouting, and milling around. Police were just beginning to appear. He got a phone call.

"Yes. The final objective has been terminated. Jota got suspicious; he checked the entire parking lot and almost saw us. Somehow he worked out that we were following him or suspected it at least. We had to hide. We've lost him again for now. Uh-huh. Yes, fine."

He turned to the others.

"Let's forget about Jota for now. The girl's hiding at her father's place. Go get her. I need to call the boss. We're almost done. Call me as soon as you have her."

"What if her uncle's there?"

"I don't give a shit. Take advantage of the commotion in the street; no one's going to come looking for us. We need to finish this today. We're going to tidy things up once and for all. It's been going on too long—we're attracting a lot of attention. Too much exposure."

Richard and one of the young men got into the Focus. The car sped off, turning right out of the parking lot. Jota, parked a prudent distance away, started up his car and began to follow the Focus. He'd been right. Sometimes the only way to catch a rat was to drive it out of its nest. After some time he realized where they were going and turned off, parking on the next street over. He got to the corner in time to see Richard and his companion get out and head for Diego's shop. Once they were there, Richard slipped down an alley while the other man waited at the door. Richard. Richard. Jota's mind was raging. He'd been with them right from the start. Fucking Richard, all these years of favors, everything Richard owed him—none of it was worth anything. He soon had the door open from the inside. Jota knew who they were after. His temples and jugular throbbed and pounded with adrenaline. He was looking out at the world through flames. One mistake, a second's delay, might cost Laura her life. He went down the same alley Richard had gone down and climbed in through the same window.

Inside, under the stairs, he found that a door had been forced open. He headed through it into the storage area with his knife in hand. He felt around in the darkness and found a candlestick, which he hefted as an auxiliary weapon. Then he crept over to the door to the office and saw a figure searching for something. He was just about to hit him when he heard Richard's voice. His former friend came back in from another room, holding a torch.

"She's not here. She might have gone out—we'll wait."

Richard inadvertently shone his torch into Jota's face, dazzling him. They both froze for a moment, and the other man took advantage of the pause to leap for Jota. He hit Jota with something that knocked him to the ground and then tried to subdue him. Jota turned over, wielding the knife, and got the man in the arm. Then he was struck again with a metal tray. Jota bucked and wriggled to get away but was kicked in the back. Then he turned again and plunged the knife into his attacker's knee. The man squealed and took out a gun. Before he could aim, Richard wrapped fishing wire around his partner's neck. The man tried to resist, but Richard was stronger. He lifted his partner up, and the man began to kick and shudder. Jota just about got his eyes open to see what was going on. The man stopped struggling, and Richard dropped him to the floor like a sack of potatoes. As he turned back to Jota, he was hit hard in the face and knocked to the ground.

Richard regained consciousness: his face was spattered with blood. He stared at Jota incredulously, still woozy from the blow. Then he realized that he was tied up. He tried to speak but initially had some difficulty. "Hey, wha-what . . . what the hell? What the fuck are you doing?"

"You broke into my home! My home!"

"It wasn't personal. It was just business."

Jota hit him again. "You were going to kill her!"

"And now I've saved you. This had nothing to do with you. I don't owe you anything. Get out."

Jota lit a cigarette.

"Aren't you going to offer me one?"

Jota gave him a drag of his.

Richard exhaled, saying, "This is your last chance to get out of this alive. We're even. Never come back to the gym; it'll be better for the both of us. Now get out of here. I'm giving you that."

"The girl isn't here. Why did you come?"

"Listen, Jota. No one knows you're here with me. Get out—they won't come after you. You know I don't lie. If you stay, I'll have to kill you."

"Did you kill Diego?"

"Yes."

"Were you in this right from the start?"

"Yes, Rodrigo kept me away when he put a watch on my gym, but he had to end it to keep control in the neighborhood. Tensions are running high."

"Who hired you?"

"Morgades. Your friend Clarita Morgades. I never stopped working for her. She plays dirty. She likes to intimidate people, so she sends a lot of work my way. She had a client with a very difficult job for her. At first it looked like it was about getting rid of a couple of guys, professionals. It wasn't easy. We had to get information about their partners, but we couldn't, and their contact had died by chance. That meant that the next part of the job was screwed up, and they had no fucking idea what to do. Morgades told me that they'd taken over two years to find them, and suddenly they were back where they started. All they had was the stolen lot, and all they knew about it was that it had been sold in Madrid."

"And you thought that you could get to them through the lot."

"Morgades was able to pay a lot of money . . . I was the one who told her to go to you. I told her that if she wanted to find the original lot, you were the man for the job. She loved the idea. She knew you could do it, and that would be it. But it didn't occur to me that you are enough of a bastard not to even bother looking for it."

"You wanted to use me as a hound to track down some thieves and then kill me?"

"Nothing was supposed to happen to you. Think about it. You were supposed to do your job, and then you'd collect your money. When did you ever worry about what happened to your suppliers?"

"Then Diego butted in . . ."

"That was a surprise. He went to Morgades to show her that he had the original clock so he could steal your sale. He sent her a photograph."

"Did he send it through Raul?"

"Yeah, he was the delivery boy. He and Diego had to be dealt with quickly; it was getting too dangerous. Then when Diego's daughter got into it, everything went to hell."

"Where is she?"

"She called Morgades today to sell her the clock. They arranged to meet here. She should have arrived a while ago."

"She was never coming. She's not that stupid. Were you going to kill her?"

Richard didn't answer.

"How much is her life worth, Richard? What do I have to pay to save her?"

"That's nonnegotiable."

"If you won't give her to me, I'll go to Morgades."

"You'll never stop, will you? She's a dead girl walking; whether it happens today or tomorrow doesn't matter. There's nothing you can do. You'll only get yourself killed. This has gone too far. Listen to me: she's not her mother."

"I have to go. I'm going to finish tying you up—please don't give me any trouble."

"I'm giving you a chance. Next time I'll have to kill you."

"Then I'll try to make sure we never meet again."

Jota finished binding Richard's feet with packing tape. Then he gave Richard a last puff.

"You know you're going to die, don't you? You won't be coming back. Is she really worth it?"

Jota didn't answer. He gagged the man's mouth, picked up the dead man's gun, and left. Then he clumsily dialed Laura's number. To his surprise, she picked up.

"I thought you were never going to call."

"Laura! Fucking hell! Where are you?"

"I have the clock."

"What? What do you mean?"

"It was Clara Morgades—she's responsible. My dad didn't sell the clock to anyone. He had it and offered it to her. So she killed him."

"I know that, but where are you now? Where have you gone?"

"You know where. I'm here to get my revenge."

Jota screamed at her not to do a thing, to wait for him; she wasn't ready to do what she was thinking of doing; this was exactly the wrong move. But she'd stopped listening. He hung up the phone and knew that he didn't have a choice. He had to find her as fast as he could. He raced across the city and got to Morgades's gallery sooner than he'd expected. The turmoil in his neighborhood and the pressure released by the unrest and demonstrations seemed a long way away. Here, everything was calm and quiet. Night had fallen, and the stores were closing. He saw that the lights were still on. He checked the gun, adjusted his tattered jacket with his other hand, and went inside.

The secretary looked up from his desk, surprised to see him. "Oh, it's you. We're just about to close."

The gleam from the candlestick, still coated in Richard's blood, caught the secretary's eye. He stood up in alarm. "What's going on? I'll call the—"

He didn't get to finish his sentence. Jota knocked him back with a savage blow to the head, and the man fell over his chair. Blood began to flow freely from his skull. He tried to pull himself back up, but Jota pitilessly hit him again just as hard in the neck. The fire was all he had left. The man fell limply to the floor. Jota went back to the front door and locked it from the inside. Then he heard someone come running up behind him.

Clara Morgades had come out of her office. She'd seen what had happened and couldn't take her eyes off her secretary's body. Finally, she looked up at Jota. "Is he dead?"

"I don't know. Maybe."

Morgades tried to run back into her office, but Jota was quicker and brought her down. Then he sat on top of her and punched her.

"Where's the girl?"

"What girl? What are you talking about? Just hold on for a second—"

Jota hit her again. Blood pumped from her nose.

"Wa-wait a moment. We can talk."

Jota hit her again. One of Morgades's eyes began to swell up, and she started to cough. Her tears mingled with the blood on her face. "No, no, wa-wait, please! Ugh." She gagged on her blood. "They're going to kill her! Let me make a call, I have to stop them. They're going to kill her!"

"Where?"

"At her father's shop."

Jota felt the rage running through him go up a notch. He grabbed her by the hair and punched her twice more. Morgades shook and started to cry in panic. She could barely say a word.

"Where is she?"

"She's there. Don't kill me, please. Please don't kill me . . ."

"She's here!"

Morgades cringed at his scream. She began to stammer. "No, I swear—I don't know . . . don't kill me."

Just then Jota realized what he was doing. He stood up, looked at his raw fist and the tooth chip on the floor. Morgades was covering her mangled face.

"Come on. Clean yourself up."

She got unsteadily to her feet, and he walked her to the bathroom, where she started to splash water on her face.

"Now start talking."

"The girl called me this afternoon saying she had the clock and wanted to sell it. She wanted to meet at her father's shop. I thought it was because her uncle was there."

"So you sent Richard."

"No, I don't send anyone. I called my client. He takes care of everything."

"Who is he?"

"You don't know him. Let's go to my office; I can give you his information."

"What's the clock really worth?"

"I don't know. I don't care. Any of the pieces in the lot would have been fine. I never lied to you. It was the lot that was important and the people that led us to it."

"So you could kill them."

"No, that was my client's decision. They didn't kill everyone, though. I don't know why."

"How many people have they killed?"

"I don't know. Six, maybe."

They went into the office. Morgades wrote an address down on a sheet of paper. "Here, he's here. This is his telephone number. Now you have everything. But he'll kill you."

"And you don't know where the girl is?"

"I told you we set up an ambush. She must be dead by now. You didn't let me call."

"She's smarter than you think. I want you to call your client. Tell him you have the clock and that he needs to come here."

"He never comes. My secretary's never even seen him. He's very secretive."

"Where do you meet?"

"We don't. He's an odd man."

"But if you had the clock, he'd have to see you. Where?"

"He has a place in the country—"

"Call him."

"It might be too late."

"But if you'd got the clock, you would have called him immediately?"

"Yes . . . I suppose so."

"Then call him. Tell him that you need to see him in half an hour at the usual place, that you can't talk over the phone."

"What about the girl?"

"He'll have to answer to her."

Jota locked the door from the outside. Then he heard a voice.

"Did you kill her?" it said quietly.

He turned around to see Laura with a box in her hands, looking at him with her big, childish eyes.

"Who?"

"H-her . . ."

"No. You can kill her if you like. I won't stop you."

"She killed my father!"

"That's why you goaded me into coming here. So that I would think you were dead and kill her myself."

"You would have done so before!"

"Maybe, but not for you. It's too late for that."

She collapsed to the ground. From there she held up the clock like a child showing someone a gift.

He took it and inspected it contemptuously. "It's true—it really is worthless. Anyway, she was just another pawn. She didn't order your father killed."

"Do you know who did?" Laura looked up when she spoke to him and stared at the hand holding the clock. Her expression changed as she came to a serious realization. Suddenly she seemed to be aware of the danger. "Your hand is a mess! They hurt you."

He ignored her. "I'm going to try to find out. I'm going to try to bring this whole thing to an end if I can."

"Where are you going? What are you going to do?"

"Find the man who's really behind all this. You want me to kill him?"

"No, I don't want you to! I don't want you to go. Stay with me. We'll go away; we have his clock. Let's just get out of here, please. If we go now, they'll never find us. You have friends, and I . . ."

"Now you want us to run away together? Just a moment ago you were asking me to kill for you."

"This is different. Don't go now, please. This is different. You're hurt. Don't leave me now. Please."

"You stay here. I don't want you getting in any more danger. I'll send help. They'll take you to the police station. Tell them everything, the whole story. You'll be safe there."

"Then you come too."

"You were right: the police can't fix this. Go into the shop. There's a man and a woman tied up in there. They're locked away. They won't give you any trouble."

"No, please, stay with me."

She got up to hug him and wouldn't let go. For a few moments, the hug turned into something more.

Eventually, he started to speak without looking at her. "They didn't break up because of me. That's not the story. She wasn't in love with me."

"I know, but I am."

They stayed together without moving. For a moment the fire died down, and the scar stopped throbbing. The pain disappeared. It was the power the girl had over him. In the end, he pulled away and got into the car with the clock.

"I'll be back."

The car pulled away. She watched him go with a melancholy premonition in her heart.

As he drove, Jota made a call.

"Police station, captain's office."

"Hello, it's Jota. I'd like to talk to Rodrigo."

"Good evening, Jota. It's José, his assistant. I don't know where he is right now—the neighborhood's gone to hell. All our forces are out. I don't know when I'll be able to get in touch with him."

"José, I need you to give him a message. It's very important. It's urgent. I know how things are, but this is a matter of life and death. Tell him that I have the girl, Diego's daughter, and that I know who's behind all this. Give him this address, please."

"But I don't know when he'll be back."

"Give it to him anyway. Thanks, José."

He dialed the phone again, still driving. Adolfo picked up.

"Hello."

"I know that I swore I'd never get you into this again, but I need one last favor. It's the last, I promise, but you have to do this for me. I tried to get in touch with Rodrigo, but I can't find him. I have Laura. I need you to pick her up and take her to the police station. Nothing more. I need to know that she's safe. I left her at Morgades's gallery. It's only a matter of time before they find her."

Jota drove out of the city, heading for the wealthy commuter towns to the west. Driving along empty, pristine roads, he passed properties that grew larger and farther apart with every mile. He drove along stone walls, past gated driveways and glowering security guards. Following the directions he'd been given, he turned off the main road and came to a dirt track. The car went on through an open gate onto a large estate, just as he'd expected. Jota drove for a few minutes more, the car kicking up a huge cloud of dust until it got to a clearing where a parked Bentley was waiting. He tucked the gun into his pocket and waited for a sign before getting out. A window lowered in the rear of the other car, and a man of about sixty peered out. He was thickset and completely bald and had a grave, rather amused air.

"You must be Jota. I have to admit I've come to admire you. You do good work."

"How did you know I was coming?"

"I've known Clara long enough to be able to read between the lines. She called to tell me she had the clock. Who else could it be?"

"Yes, I've got the clock."

"Aha, that's very good news. Then I suppose you're here to come to some kind of arrangement."

The client calmly stepped out of the car. His body matched his face: he was short and squat with a large belly and short legs, a tailored jacket, cufflinks, and a tiepin, all in excellent taste. A proud man without a hint of humility.

"Why don't we talk like human beings? Speaking into a car makes me feel a little ridiculous, as though I were a policeman. I believe we're both acting in good faith, and we're both men of business, aren't we?"

Jota got out at the man's invitation. The driver's door of the Bentley opened, and the blond man got out as well.

"This is my driver—don't worry. He's part of the family." The client went over to Jota and shook his hand warmly. "Remember: I didn't know if you were coming alone either. Really, I'd much rather have done this deal over a good dinner. We still can, if you like? It would be my pleasure."

"No, I want to get this over with."

"Shall we take a walk? Don't worry; he'll stay here. Don't bother getting the clock. He won't steal it while we're gone. After all, you have a gun or the kind of weapon men like you keep hidden somewhere on your person. I run the greater risk by far. He won't search you or anything. I want you to be comfortable, to understand that this is absolutely between us. That's the only way to do a deal."

"I'd like to bring it with me anyway."

"Whatever makes you most comfortable. Do you mind if I ask you about your work?"

"No."

They walked off under the blond man's gaze, talking calmly, along a forest path.

"I'm glad to have the chance to get a good look at you. I need to meet people in person to know whether I can trust them or not. That's essential in my world. Now we can discuss the price. I've been thinking long and hard about it. You know how it is in business: it's a very fine line that one has to tread if you want both parties to walk away feeling that they haven't been cheated. The exact right price at which you feel that it was worth it and I feel that I haven't paid too much. I've been doing deals for forty years, and believe me—it's the most sensitive issue. Most deals fall apart after the agreement has been reached, when one of the parties has had time to think and decides that they've been swindled. It's so awful when that happens . . ."

"Whenever someone starts talking like this, I know they're going to try to screw me anyway."

The man laughed, saying, "You're very wise, but that's not true in this case. You haven't thought it through. You don't just have the clock; you have a lot of information too. I can't let you walk away from this dissatisfied. Just as I can't let you go away thinking this is a bottomless well to which you can return whenever you like. Do you understand?"

"Perfectly."

"Thank you. So give me a price that will leave you satisfied, one that takes into account the clock and all the work you've put in, including the aggravation. But be fair; if you're trying to cheat me, I'll know."

"I want the girl. That's the price."

"These things always turn up surprises. I'm sorry. There's nothing I can do about that now."

"You're wrong. Your other 'driver' didn't get to her. It seems she's not as stupid as you think."

"I would never think such a thing. Do you know where she is?"

"Safe. But I want to know that when I leave, she'll be as safe as I am."

"You're asking for the only thing I can't give you."

"Why? Why me and not her?"

"Because you can name a price."

"So can she! I can do the deal on her behalf."

"Now you're the one trying to cheat me."

"Not at all. I'll take her away with me, and you'll never see her again. Why can't you leave her alone?"

"Because I understand her. You don't. You don't understand at all. Do you want to know the true value of the clock? Give it to me. Come on; don't worry. After all, I'm going to buy it from you anyway."

Jota handed it over.

The man looked at it affectionately. "Yes, I remember it from when I was little . . ."

Then he dropped it top-side down. It smashed. Jota didn't move.

"The material value of things isn't what's important, but one only learns that when they've already got everything they've ever wanted. When you achieve your goals, you learn to look at things from a different perspective. My father was a very good man who taught me that from a young age. It's thanks to him that I got to where I am today. A man who started out with a little store and worked every day to make sure that we'd never want for anything. But he was never rich, not like me. He only ever had enough to live day to day. He never even had his own home or owned any property. We've gone quite far. We should be heading back.

"As I was saying. In the end, all he wanted to do was retire to a little house with my mother, a little house that, thank God, I was able to give them. But none of that mattered to the bastards who broke in to rob them. They were just a harmless elderly couple who never hurt anyone, and some animals broke into their home one night to steal from them. Do you know what the police said? That if the thieves hadn't gone upstairs to their room, they would have slept right through it. You understand? They could have taken what they wanted, and nobody would have been hurt. But no, these beasts wanted more. They didn't just want to steal from them what little they had. They went up to the bedroom and woke my father just for the fun of it. He wasn't a cowardly man, so he tried to face them down: they pulled him out of bed and started to hit his head against the floor while my mother watched. Again and again and again, dragging him around, letting him try to get up and hitting him again. He lost an eye. He was still conscious, but they didn't stop. They smacked him against the floor until he stopped moving. And they made my mother watch. When his head was nothing but a bloody mess, they pulled him up and threw his body on top of her as though they were . . . just for fun . . . then they went for her. They beat her to death. They didn't leave off until she'd stopped breathing. They didn't give her a moment's respite. She suffered horribly. But my father was still alive when the ambulance arrived. He was a very tough man. They tortured him, they left him mortally wounded, but still they made him watch his wife die. He finally passed away at the foot of his bed, like a dog. Such cruelty and violence . . . inconceivable. It didn't take me long to see that the legal system wouldn't be enough. They couldn't even find the men responsible."

"I'm sorry."

"Thanks to a friend in the force, I was able to track down one of the murderers, and that was when I realized that all my wealth and power meant nothing if I couldn't wield them to levy justice where the law was unable to."

"So you decided to get your revenge on the thieves."

"This wasn't just about simple revenge. The guilty weren't just those who committed the brutal crime. Everyone who earned some kind of benefit out of it is equally to blame. Those who don't ask questions, the hypocrites who take the money and look the other way, who hide behind their false ignorance."

"You gave orders to kill everyone who got something out of the crime?"

"Only those who benefited directly. The people whose hands were just as dirty as the murderers themselves. The moneylenders who make their living from other people's crimes, who propagate evil and impunity. I've known plenty in my time. Would you have done any different in my place?"

"I don't know."

"I don't expect you to understand me. You may only be interested in the financial side of things, but I know that I have arranged for justice to be done."

"I never like to be so sure of myself. What about the girl?"

"I understand her; she's just as wounded as I am. That's how I know that I'll never be able to come to an arrangement with her, and I'm sorry about that. Believe me—I am. I understand her, but you don't."

"You've killed her father! You made her suffer just as you did! Where's the justice in that?"

"That's different: my parents were innocent."

"We're all victims and executioners."

"I was wrong about you, wasn't I? You don't care about the money, just the girl. Isn't that right? Maybe you understand better than I thought. Deep down, you and I share the same collector's spirit. We have done what we've done for a past that will never come back to thank us. But she's already dead."

Then Jota heard another car arrive and saw headlights moving through the clearing, casting ghostly shapes: long, irregular shadows. He saw that he'd fallen into a trap and pointed his gun at the client, dragging him back toward him.

The black Ford Focus had parked between the other two cars. One of its doors was open, but two figures could still be seen inside. Jota looked for the blond man: he'd disappeared.

"Why won't you listen to me? She can't be saved. It's a shame. I assure you that it saddens me. I thought that you'd come to an agreement, but I suppose that the older we get, the more foolish we are."

"You and I are leaving. If your men try anything . . ."

"Is this the gentleman who was supposed to take care of her while you were talking to me?"

Two figures emerged from the Focus: the first was one of the client's thugs. The other was Adolfo. He was devastated. He couldn't look Jota in the eye.

Suddenly, Jota shuddered involuntarily and fell down. The blond man had sneaked up behind him and shocked him with a Taser. Jota curled up on the ground while the blond man and the bodyguard dragged their boss toward the Bentley.

"Is it done?" the client asked, feigning distress.

"Yeah. The girl too."

"Awful, just awful."

They both got into the car and drove away, followed by the Focus. The blond man stayed behind, watching Jota in amusement as he crawled along the ground, trying to get up. He let him be for a few moments until Jota managed to get up onto his knees; then he came over and kicked him in the ribs and face, playing with him like a cat does with a mouse. Jota tried to put some distance between them, but the blond man just kicked him harder. When Jota couldn't move anymore, he curled up into a ball, but the blond man turned him over, laughing.

"Come on! You're not going to give up so soon, are you? Don't disappoint me!"

He walked over to stamp on his face, but Jota—letting the fire take over—thrust upward as hard as he could. The man let out a wild scream and stepped back, looking at his groin. A red patch spread as blood spurted. When he saw where the wound was, he got dizzy. Jota dragged himself over to the gun and fired three times, although he only hit the man once. He was nothing but flames. The blond man fell to the ground in agony, but Jota ignored him. He got up. His face was disfigured, but he used the good eye he had left to inspect the tracks the cars had left behind and stumbled over to his own, trying not to think of Laura. He couldn't let himself panic. "It's just the fire. Let it take you," he muttered to himself. He finally reached his car and searched his pockets as though he had all the time in the world. The keys. He could barely see through the veil of blood; his left eye was swollen shut. He leaned on the door, unable to stay upright, and forced himself to get in. Laura. Laura was in danger; he needed to find her. He was pure flame. He sat down, put the gun between his legs, and inserted the key in the ignition. But he hadn't seen the shadow waiting in the back seat to help the blond man dispose of the body. Now the shadow was going to finish the job. Richard wrapped a cable around Jota's neck so he could strangle him without seeing his face, staring into the distance as he did so. He didn't want to kill Jota, but his friend had gone too far. Richard felt Jota's hands grab his arms, trying to pull the cable away from his neck to get some air. But he wouldn't last much longer; the cable was drawing blood. Richard felt the right arm go limp, but he didn't see it reach between Jota's legs, pick up the gun, and point it backward, resting it on his shoulder. Richard only noticed it pointing erratically at his head when it was too late. As the warm barrel waved a couple of inches from his face, he only had time to murmur.

"No—"

The shot blew away some of his skull, just above his eye, spattering the roof with blood and brains. The shock wave smashed a window and threw him backward like a rag doll. Jota was deafened; all he could hear was a buzzing sound, the buzz of all the different tones he'd never hear again. The sound was mystical somehow, becoming a kind of mantra that helped to keep him conscious. He couldn't feel the flames, the burn the pistol had left on his neck, the blood seeping from his throat, or any of his other wounds. The air filled his lungs again; he'd almost suffocated, and now he was flooded with the energy to go on, to get Laura. She was waiting for him. She couldn't be allowed to fall into their clutches.

The thought of Laura and the sight of blood dribbling down between his legs brought the pain rushing back. He was back in the horror of the moment. Suddenly he realized that he was bleeding out.

It was too late. But as his strength ebbed away, he concentrated on Laura. Laura was waiting for him—Laura, whom he'd done all this for. Laura, in the dress she always wore, lying on the grass with him one summer afternoon as they planned to run away and leave their lives behind forever.

"Don't make the same mistakes as your parents."

"I'd never do that with you."

Laura, it's not too late. It's never too late. The past twenty years without you were the worst mistake of my life, but we can fix that. Laura, let's go back to that time and decide once and for all. Who was the coward? You or me? Or both of us? Let's go back to that time, and we'll never lose David. My hands will never be stained with blood. I've paid for my mistakes; now I can love you. I can learn to be what we wanted to be. Together again. Jota smiled, happy that he'd done the right thing, no matter the cost. The pain had gone. The fire had gone out, forever. He smiled. He could smell Laura's scent again. His mind slipped back into pleasant, far-off memories like a flock of birds rising up from a field at night, leaving behind only silence and oblivion.

8

Laura was waiting in front of the gallery, fiddling with the pen without realizing it, when she saw a car's headlights. She got up and went toward it but was still cautious. The car parked, and two young men got out.

"Hello, are you Laura? Jota called us. We've come to pick you up."

"Where is he?"

"He's waiting for you. We're going to meet up with him."

The young man came over, smiling, and gently took her arm. She smiled back and promptly sprayed him in the eyes with the pepper spray. The man screamed and collapsed. His friend came over to help him while she ran down the street.

"Hey, man, are you OK?"

"Oooow! Fuck, fucking hell! Run after her, damn it. Don't let her get away."

The boy set out in pursuit. Laura ran, shouting for help as she went, but she was breathless and barely made any sound.

"Help! Help!"

She headed down a narrow one-way street full of dark offices, looking desperately for anyone who might be able to help, but there was no one around. The odd security guard may have seen her flash past, but they probably didn't realize what was going on and certainly didn't react. She felt her face going red, her breathing growing short, and the man getting closer. A set of headlights appeared behind him. The other man was driving the wrong way down the street, barely able to see. He was going to catch up with her in a second. He wanted to run her over. She jumped to the side, but the car hit her, and she rolled up onto the hood before falling to the ground, hurt. The driver kept going, laughing, but was suddenly dazzled by a light in front of him. He tried to swerve, lost control, and went right into the oncoming car. Meanwhile, his companion grabbed Laura by the hair, pulling her up. Stunned, she didn't react. They both stared into the headlights.

A surprised Rodrigo got out of the car, keeping the headlights on. His gun was drawn.

"Laura? What's going on?"

She looked up and tried to get free.

"You: let her go. Laura, come over here. What were you doing?"

They both obeyed, and she ran over to him.

"Did they hurt you? Are you OK?"

She nodded.

"Cowards, pieces of shit . . . Jota called to ask me to pick you up. I'm sorry it took me so long. The neighborhood has gone crazy. Get into the car. Don't worry; these two will get what's coming to them."

She sat in the passenger seat while he took his phone out of his jacket. He looked away, and just then the man who'd tried to run her down shot three times. Rodrigo tried to return fire but fell against the door, staring at Laura with the light fading fast from his eyes. She watched in horror.

"L-Laura . . ."

The other man grabbed his companion in terror. "Oh, fuck, fuck! What did you do? That was a fucking cop! You're crazy! Now we're truly fucked!"

"Shut up! That's it. Let's go, damn it. I'm going to fuck you up, you fucking whore."

While the other man sniveled in panic, the murderer ran toward Rodrigo's car. Laura jumped into the driver's seat just as he got to the door and tried to open it. She locked it, but the window was open. He easily reached in to unlock it.

"I'm going to get you, bitch."

Still only halfway into the driver's seat, Laura managed to put the car in reverse as fast as it would go. Her attacker tried to climb onto the chassis but fell and was dragged along a few feet until she saw him roll in front of her headlights, trying to get up. Their eyes met. He knew what was going to happen. She shifted gears and pressed down on the gas, running right over him. Then she took aim at the other man, who stared at her in terror, still standing next to the car. He tried to get in, but she kept going at full speed and caught him when he was only halfway in, smashing his body into a wall. Then she turned around to look at her other assailant and saw that he was trying to get up. She drove back toward him and pushed his body right back into the building across the street, crushing him slowly. The kid tried to push back against the chassis as though there were some chance he might make it, but soon dark liquid began to dribble from his mouth, and he lost control of his limbs before falling limp.

Laura sat in the car in silence. The engine was still running. Then she realized that the radio had been playing the whole time.

The sun was coming up. The local press was covering the disturbances that had turned the neighborhood into a battlefield the night before, but fortunately no one had been seriously hurt beyond bruised bones and several arrests. Some of the violence that had been brewing under the surface had been released, and local residents now felt lighter, as though they'd gotten rid of something that had been festering, even if it was only brief relief from a symptom of the underlying disease: a sick society. That day, counterintuitively, everyone woke up feeling better, healthier even. Finally, people were thinking twice about taking their hatred out on the most vulnerable scapegoats, and that was the real release. Spring had begun.

In the alley by Morgades's gallery, a crowd of onlookers had gathered around the police cordon. The bodies were covered. Inside an ambulance, a paramedic and a policewoman were tending to Laura, who was hugging her knees with a blanket wrapped around her.

"The psychiatric trauma unit is on its way. We've informed your mother. Don't worry. Everything's going to be OK."

"You know Jota, don't you?"

"Yes."

"You . . . you've found him, haven't you?"

The policewoman was surprised at her composure. Laura was staring at her unemotionally, with glassy eyes, and the policewoman felt she had to be honest. "No."

"What?"

"We don't know where Jota is. We found his car in the countryside with one body inside and another next to it, but he wasn't there."

Laura made an ambiguous face. The policewoman didn't know what to say; she couldn't tell what Laura was thinking.

Then Laura giggled nervously. "He won't be back."

"From where?"

"I don't know. He . . . he had a cat. I'd like to adopt it."

"Adopt it?"

"Jota's gone. He's going to miss him."

EPILOGUE

A slight groove had been worn into the middle of the imperial marble staircase, but the round banisters stood tall on either side, and in the large antechamber a string quartet was playing—not that many people were listening anymore. Most of the guests had already gone into the hall reserved for the main event.

This was an exclusive dinner for important businessmen: about a dozen tables with six to ten diners at each. Morgades's client was reading a speech of thanks from a small podium, clearly very gratified.

"Thank you very much, my friends. I really can't thank you enough for the extraordinary trust you've placed in me over the past few years, but I am sure that the challenges our companies are bound to face in the future . . ."

As he spoke, three men came in through a side door, but their way was blocked by a waiter. One of them flashed a badge, and the waiter stood aside. They asked him a question, and he pointed at the podium. Once they'd found him, they stood at the back, waiting discreetly. Nobody seemed to have noticed them. The client's tone changed.

"I'm afraid that I must bring this speech to a close, but I don't want to leave without saying something that you may never have heard me say before, and it's very important that I do before I give up this role. My dear friends: maybe the aspect of my career in the business world that I am most proud of is that I never lost track of my moral compass, as hard as that might have been sometimes . . . when you know that you must fight for something, you know that you must get to the end regardless of the consequences. Even if it means losing everything you ever had. Any damage done will be compensated for by the knowledge that you did what you had to do. Many thanks."

The guests sat in silence for a moment, surprised by these unexpected sentiments, until somebody started to clap and was immediately followed by all the others until the applause grew quite fevered. He came down amid the noise while the policemen approached him quietly.

Adolfo was sitting in his shop, staring into space. The front door opened, and Laura came in, half her face covered in bandages and various parts of her body in plaster. He didn't seem surprised. He waited until she'd sat down opposite him, across the desk. They looked at each other without a word. In the end, he spoke first.

"I thought the cops would be coming with you . . . well, it doesn't matter. They'll turn up eventually."

She didn't say anything. There was no hatred in her eyes. She seemed numb.

"Aren't you going to do anything? My wife has left me. She's taken the girls. You're too young to understand what that means, but waiting for the police is all I can do now."

"It was you, wasn't it?"

"Yes, I told them where you were."

"No, not that. Did you go get Jota? I don't understand. You're the only one it could have been, but I don't understand . . ."

"Yes, it was me. He was there, with them. I waited for them to go, and then I went back. I thought maybe I could still save him, even though I knew it was too late. But he's a very stubborn man—he'd killed them. I still can't believe it."

"Where did you take him?"

"He was badly hurt. I don't think he would have made it if I hadn't gone back. But I took him away. I can't tell you where. Fortunately, he had somewhere to go."

"Is he OK?"

"I guess. I don't know."

"Is he coming back?"

"No. He planned it all out in the past few days. He got rid of everything, even his name. Maybe you'll see him again one day. I don't know where or when, but a long time from now, when you've forgotten all about him."

"Why? Where's he gone?"

"Sometimes a new generation has to come onto the scene before an old story can come to an end. You're the new blood he needed to do that."

"But I didn't bring anything to an end. This had nothing to do with what happened to you."

"I think you taught him something. That the past isn't set in stone; you can get over things. I don't know. And now he's gone—I don't know where, but somewhere overseas, I imagine. He's going to bring a story that's been running for twenty years to a close. Come to terms with a death that has been on his conscience all this time. And earn back his name."

Laura stared at him urgently.

"I imagine that's why you're here. It's all I can give you." Jota's partner sighed. "Well, the story starts a long time ago, more than twenty years, much more, with four guys who were very close. They thought they were going to take the world by storm. They thought that things would turn out very different from how they did. But that's how all stories go: when you start out, you always think that life is going to turn out differently."

While Jota's partner told an old, painful story, light began to shine on old wounds, clearing away the rotting, stagnant air that had festered during twenty years of silence. A cat with no collar leaped gracefully into a hidden alley from a window it would never find open again, heading for places unknown, on his way to nowhere in particular.

About the Author

Photo © 2018 Laura Pacheco Castro

Guillermo Valcárcel was born in Madrid. He worked in the construction industry by day and studied filmmaking by night until 2008, when he moved to Costa Rica, where he currently lives and works as a filmmaker. He also dedicates his time to writing and illustrating. He is the author of the thrillers *Counterfeit* and *Shadows Across America* as well as *The Wave That Hit Spain*, an influential essay that launched his writing career.

About the Translator

Photo © 2018 Ar De Bonis Orquera

Kit Maude is a Spanish-to-English translator and editor based in Buenos Aires. His translations of stories by Latin American authors have been featured in *Granta*, the *Literary Review*, and the *Short Story Project*, among other publications. He has translated several great Argentinian and Uruguayan writers, including Jorge Luis Borges, Armonía Somers, Julio Cortázar, Antonio Di Benedetto, and Adolfo Bioy Casares. He was born in Hong Kong and received a bachelor's degree in comparative American studies from the University of Warwick in the United Kingdom.